Together

Read more UNICORN and YETI books!

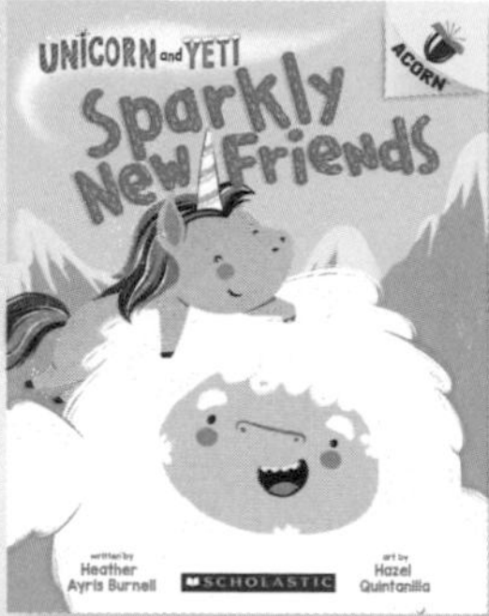
UNICORN and YETI
ACORN
Sparkly New Friends
written by Heather Ayris Burnell
SCHOLASTIC
art by Hazel Quintanilla

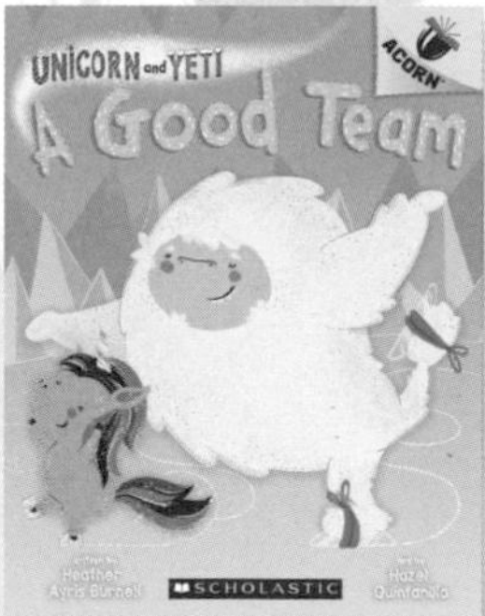
UNICORN and YETI
ACORN
A Good Team
SCHOLASTIC

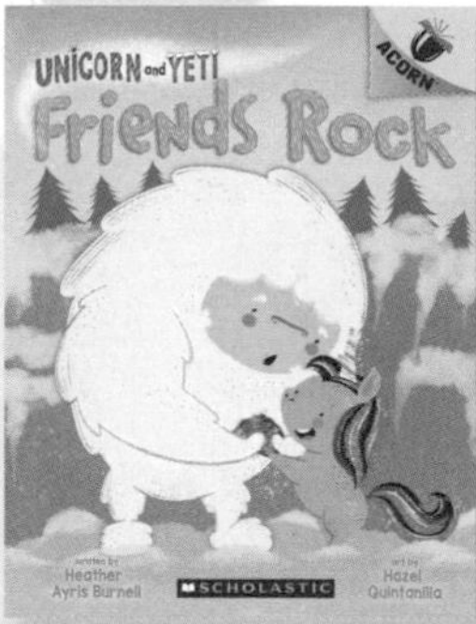
UNICORN and YETI
ACORN
Friends Rock
written by Heather Ayris Burnell
SCHOLASTIC
art by Hazel Quintanilla

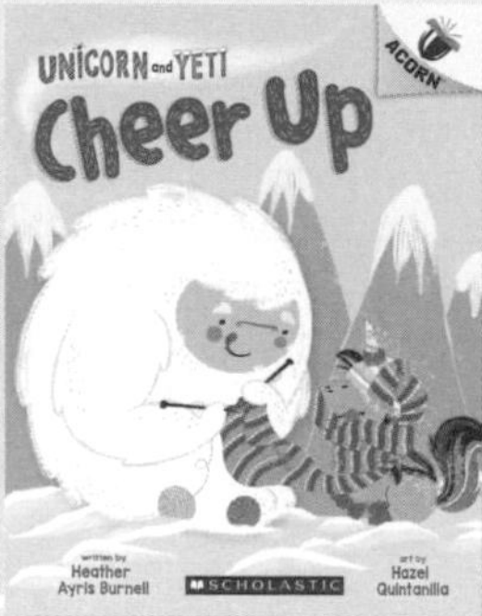
UNICORN and YETI
ACORN
Cheer Up
written by Heather Ayris Burnell
SCHOLASTIC
art by Hazel Quintanilla

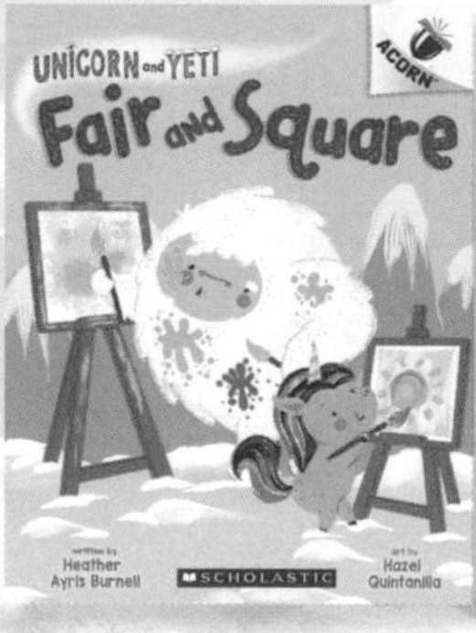
UNICORN and YETI
ACORN
Fair and Square
written by Heather Ayris Burnell
SCHOLASTIC
art by Hazel Quintanilla

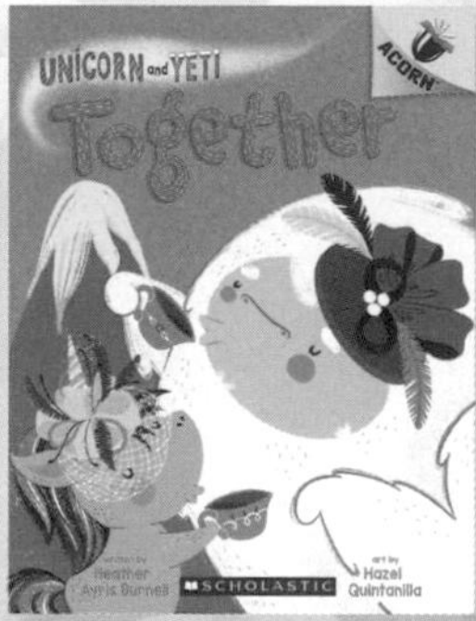
UNICORN and YETI
ACORN
Together
SCHOLASTIC
art by Hazel Quintanilla

UNICORN and YETI

Together

written by
Heather Ayris Burnell

art by
Hazel Quintanilla

ACORN™
SCHOLASTIC INC.

For Hil. We always have fun when we're together! — HAB

To my four-legged babies: Frida, Camila, Lucy, Catalina, Dante, Bruno, Luna, Jack, and Fiona, I love you. — HQ

Library of Congress Cataloging-in-Publication Data

Names: Burnell, Heather Ayris, author. | Quintanilla, Hazel, 1982-illustrator.
Title: Together / by Heather Ayris Burnell ; illustrated by Hazel Quintanilla.
Description: First edition. | New York, NY : Acorn, Scholastic Inc., 2022.|
Series: Unicorn and Yeti ; 6 | Summary: In three stories, friends
Unicorn and Yeti spend time with each other, watching clouds in the sky,
playing copycat, and having a tea party.
Identifiers: LCCN 2021001241 (print) | ISBN 9781338627756 (paperback) |
ISBN 9781338627763 (library binding) |
Subjects: CYAC: Unicorns—Fiction. | Yeti—Fiction. | Friendship—Fiction. | Humorous stories.
Classification: LCC PZ7.B92855 To 2022 (print) | DDC [E]—dc23
LC record available at https://lccn.loc.gov/2021001241 LC

10 9 8 7 6 5 4 3 2 1   22 23 24 25 26

Printed in China   62

First edition, February 2022

Edited by Katie Carella
Book design by Sarah Dvojack

Table of Contents

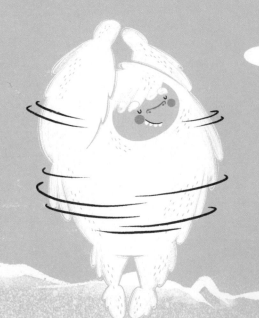

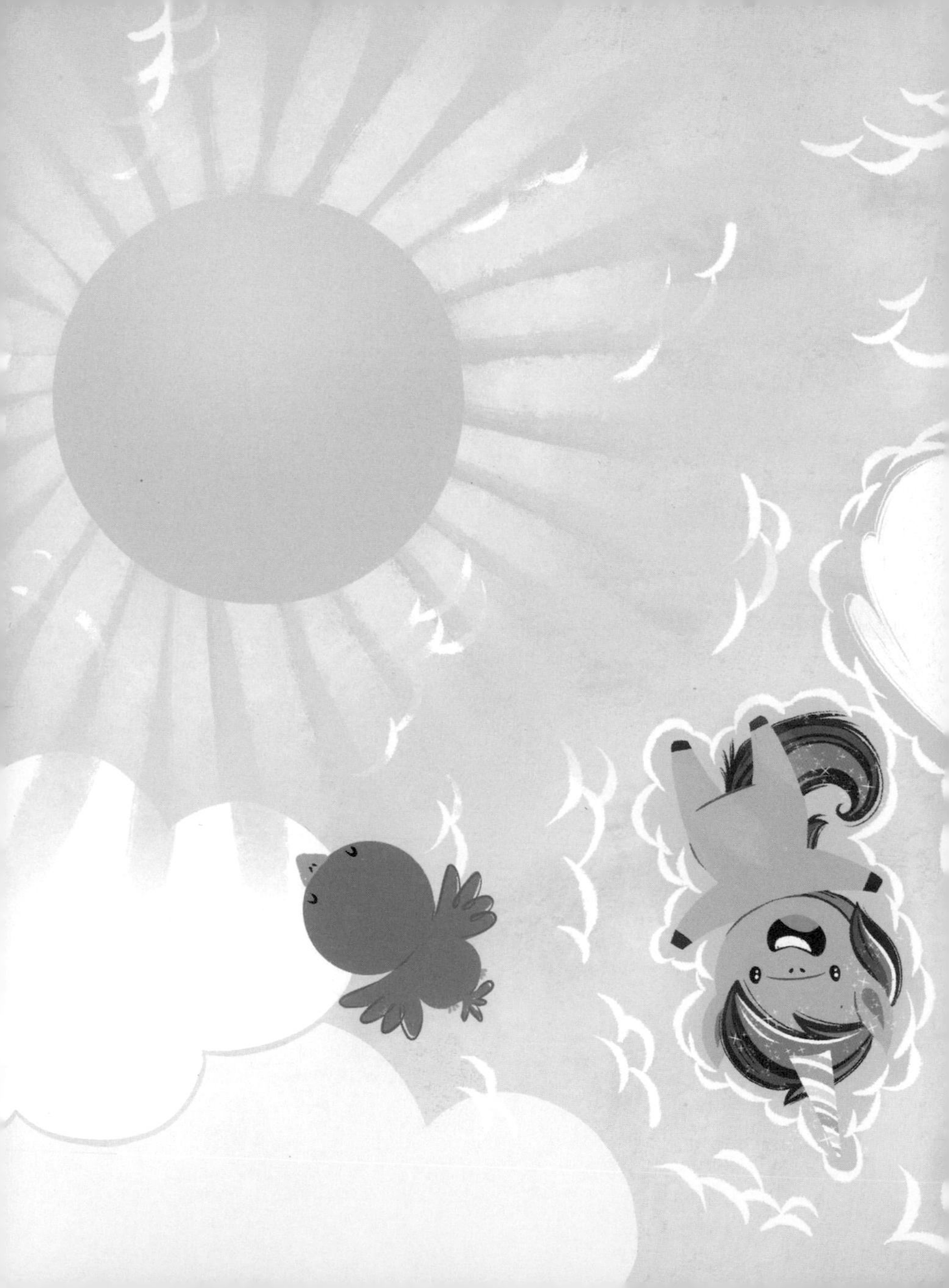

Zip! Zigzag! Zoom!

Unicorn and Yeti looked up.

Wow!

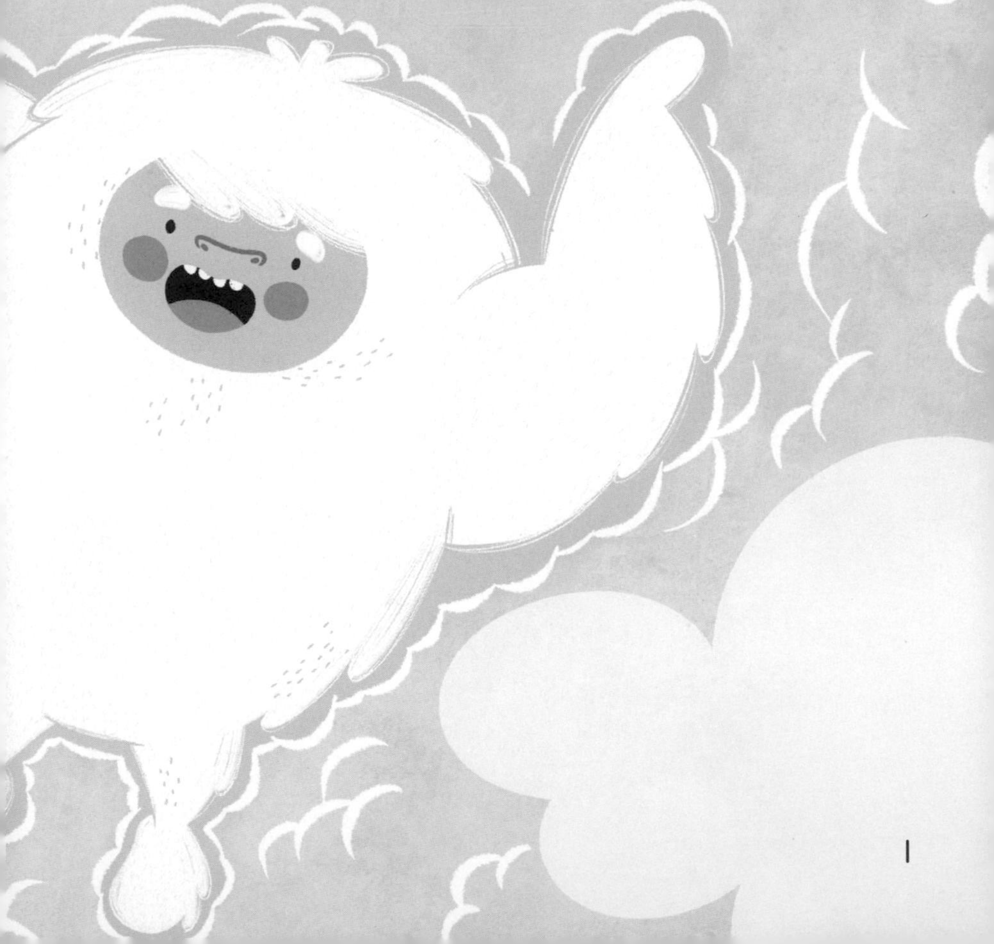

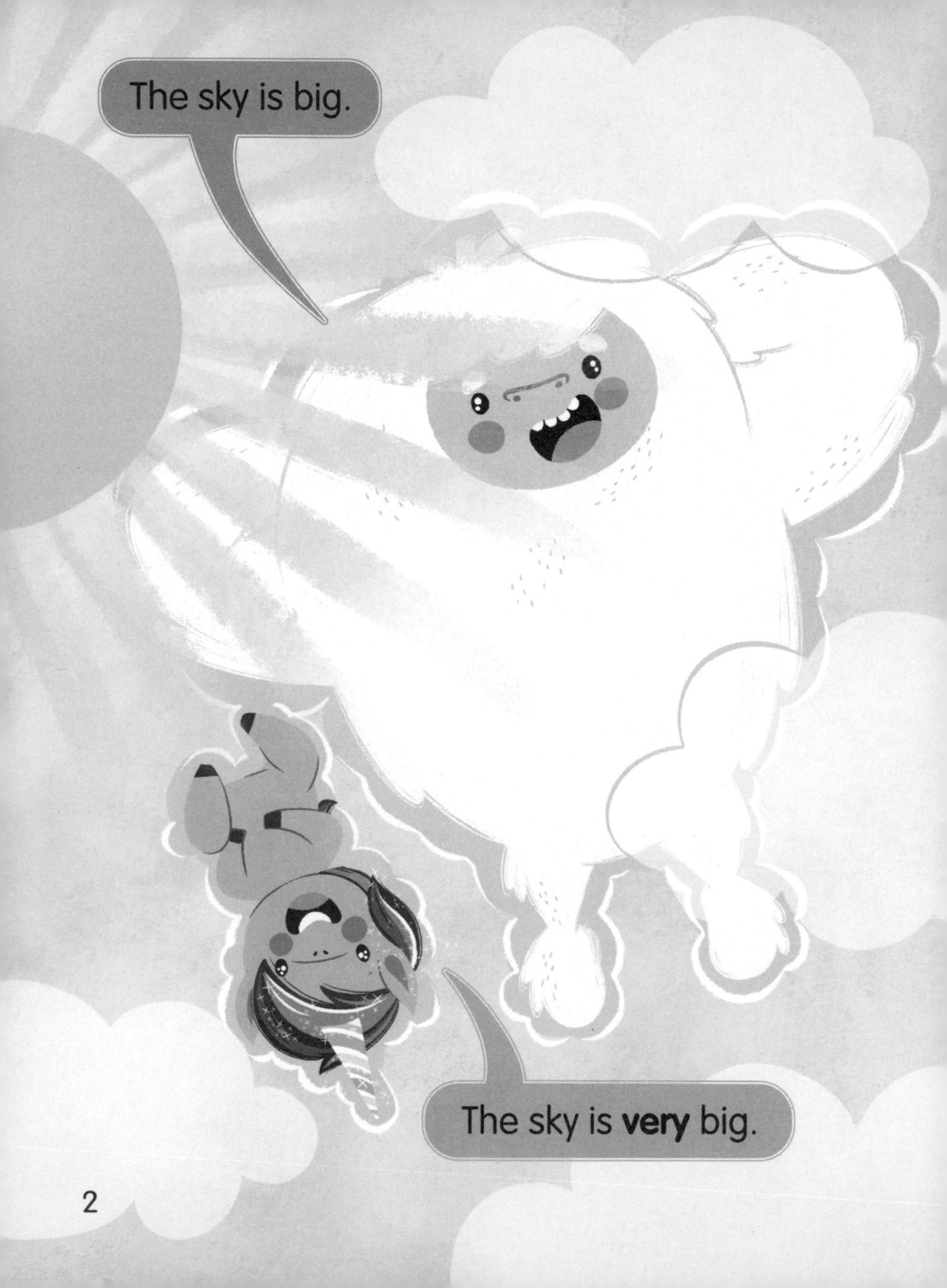
The sky is big.
The sky is **very** big.

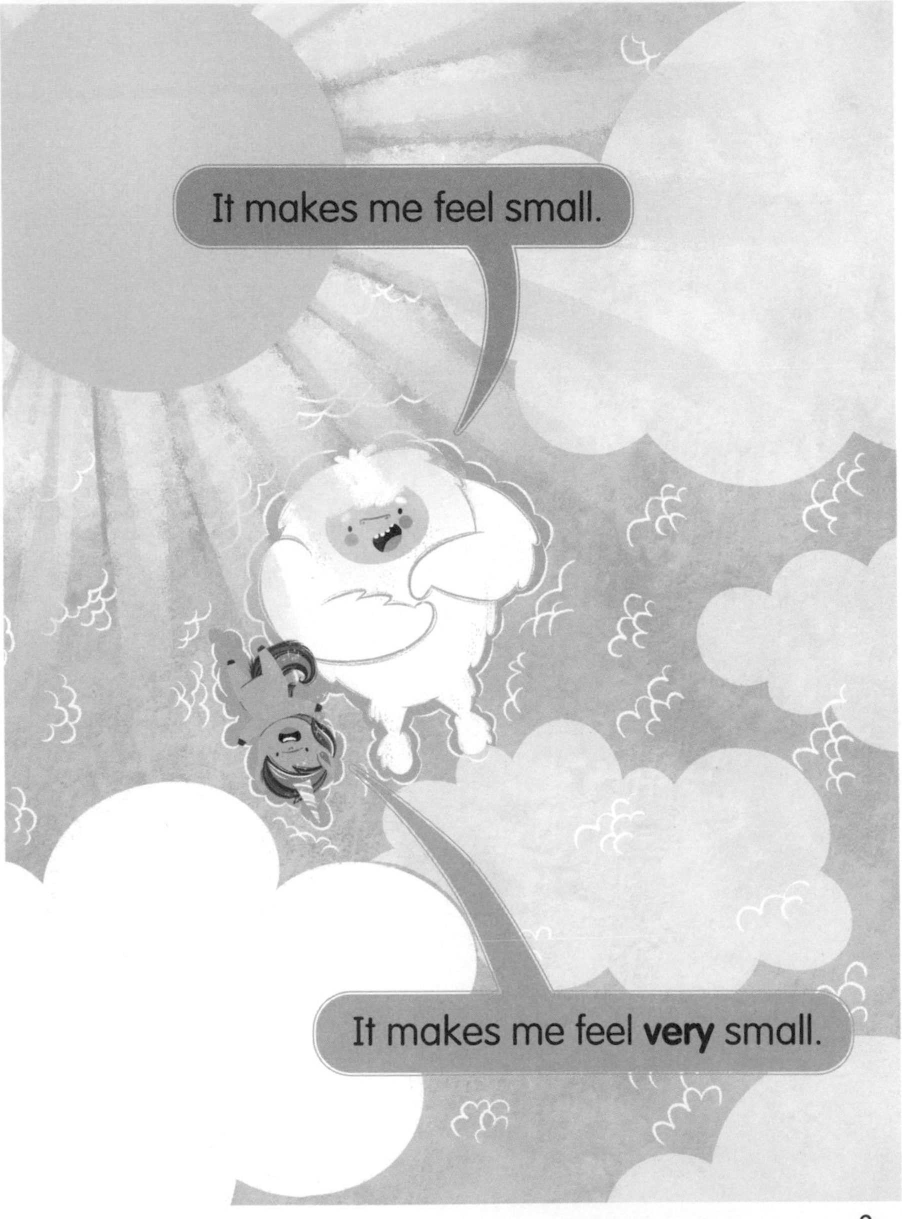
It makes me feel small.
It makes me feel **very** small.

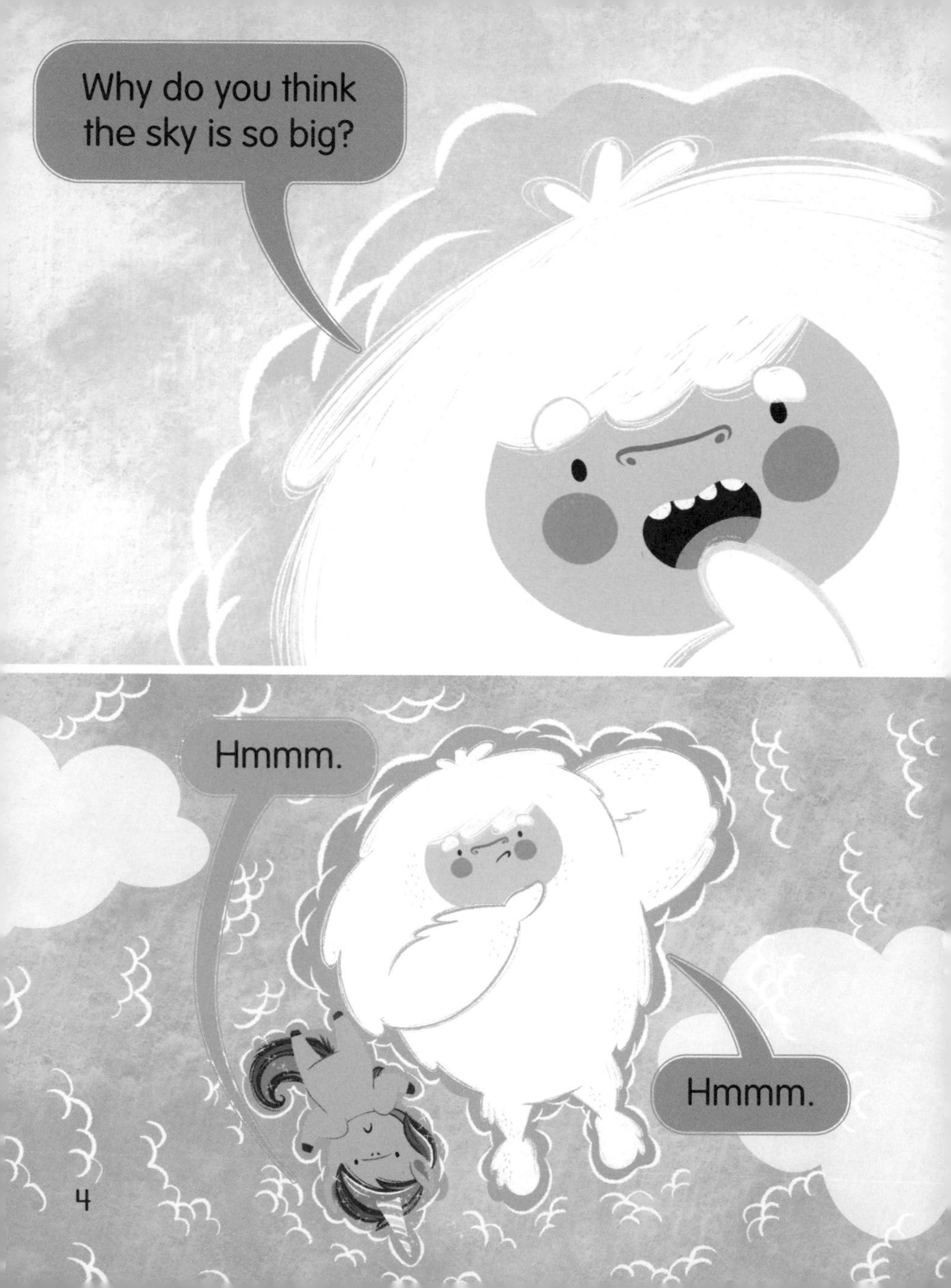
Why do you think the sky is so big?
Hmmm.
Hmmm.

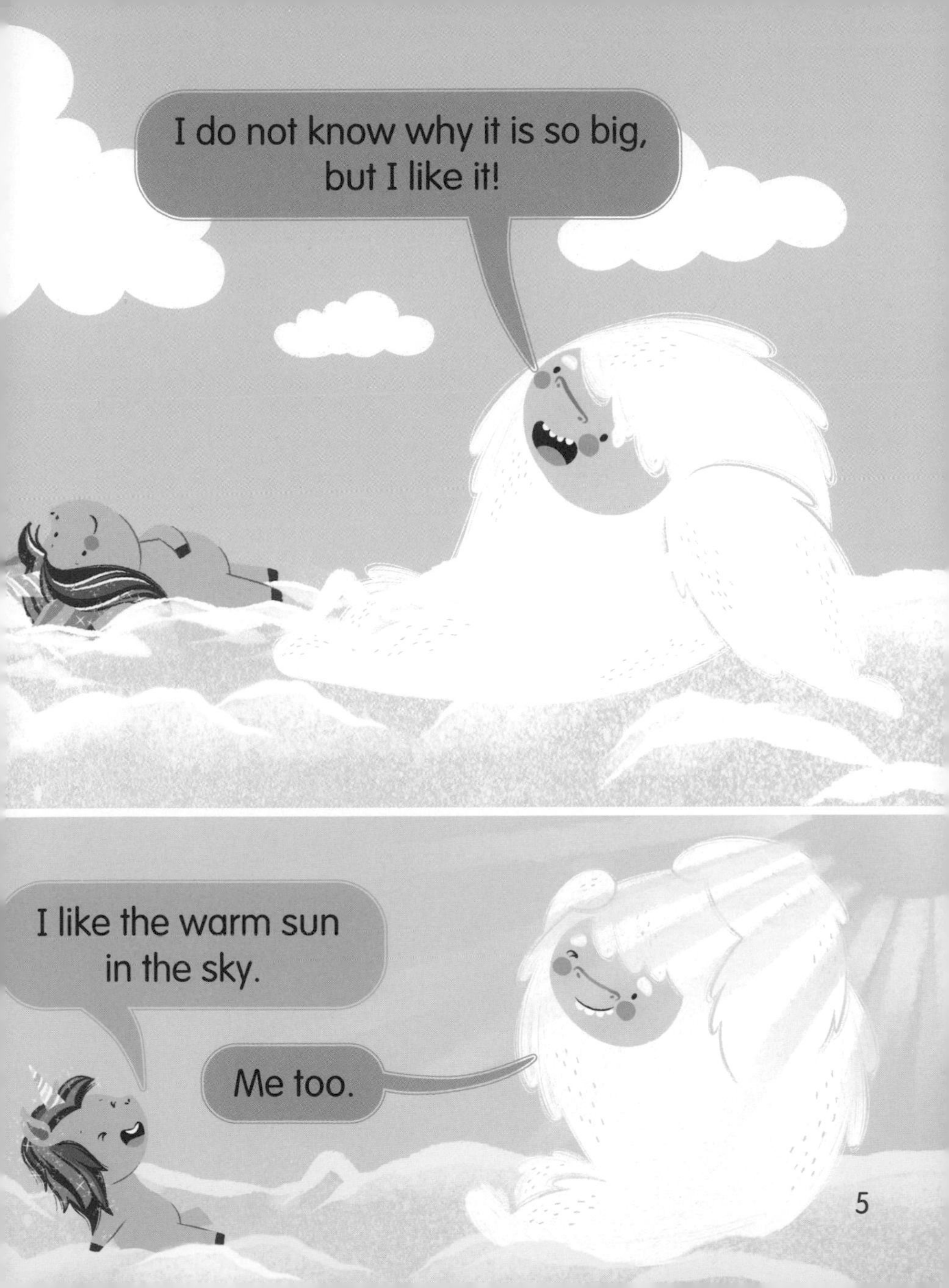
I do not know why it is so big, but I like it!
I like the warm sun in the sky.
Me too.

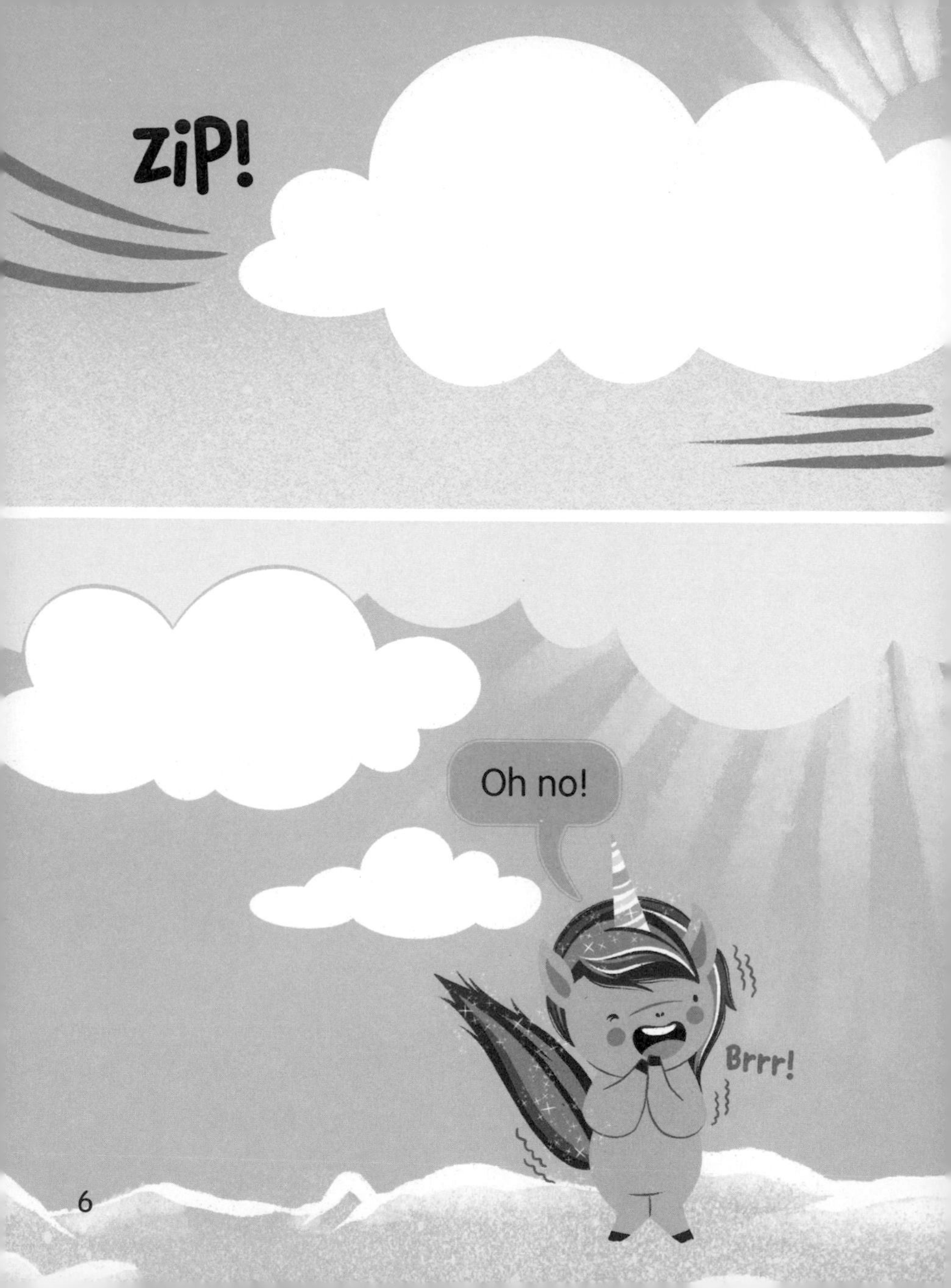
ZiP!
Oh no!
Brrr!

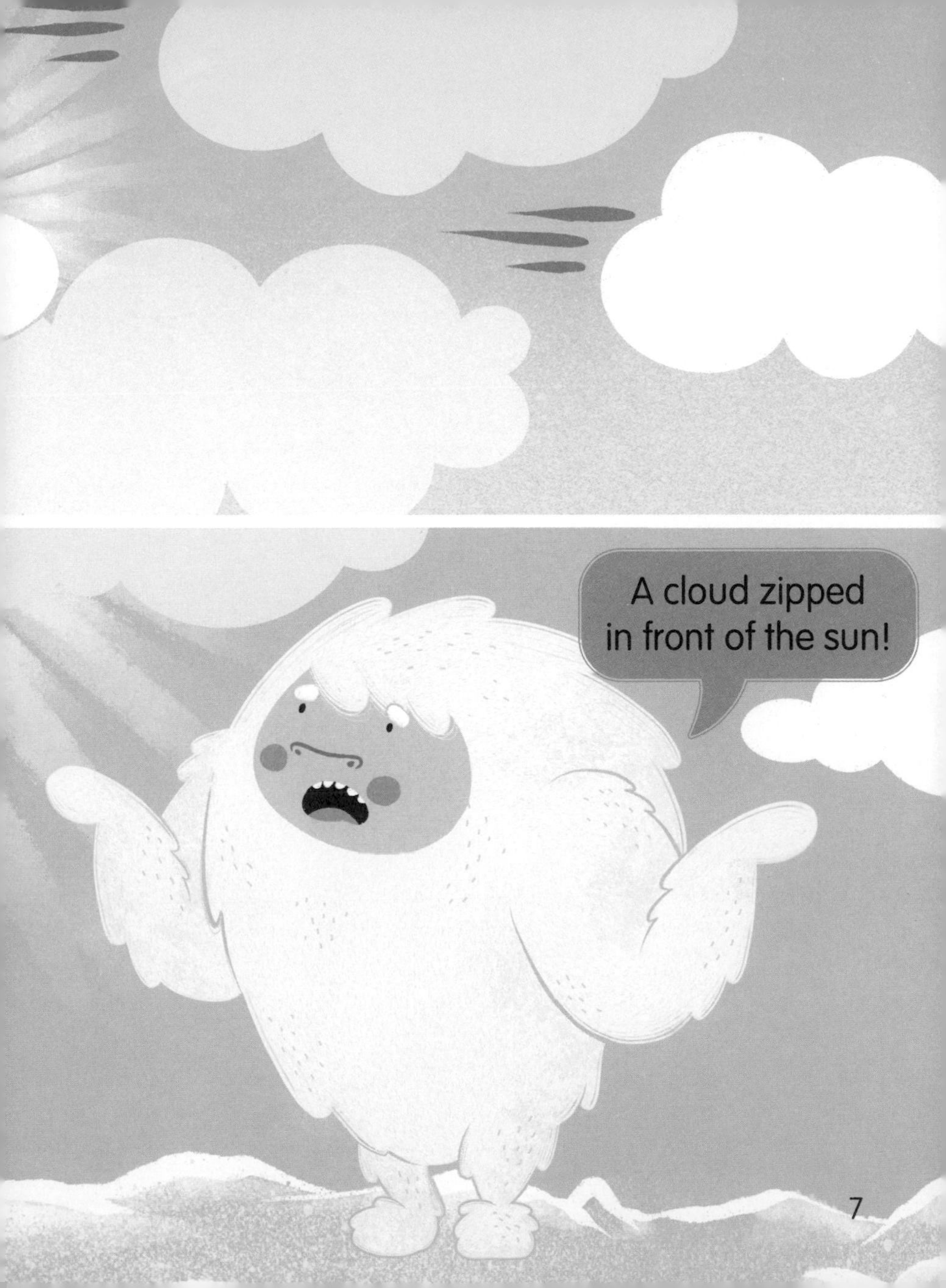
A cloud zipped
in front of the sun!

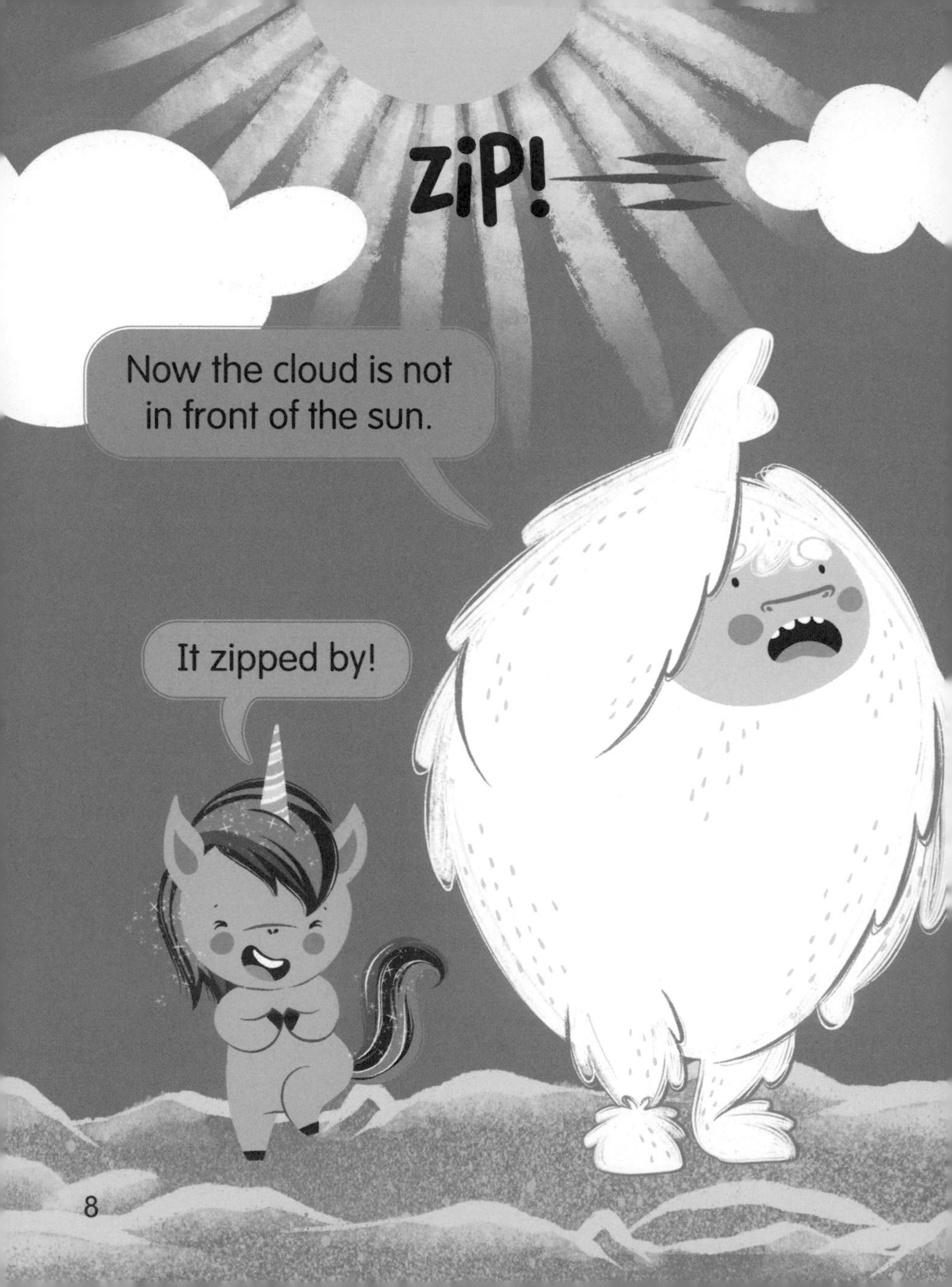

ZiP!
Now the cloud is not in front of the sun.
It zipped by!

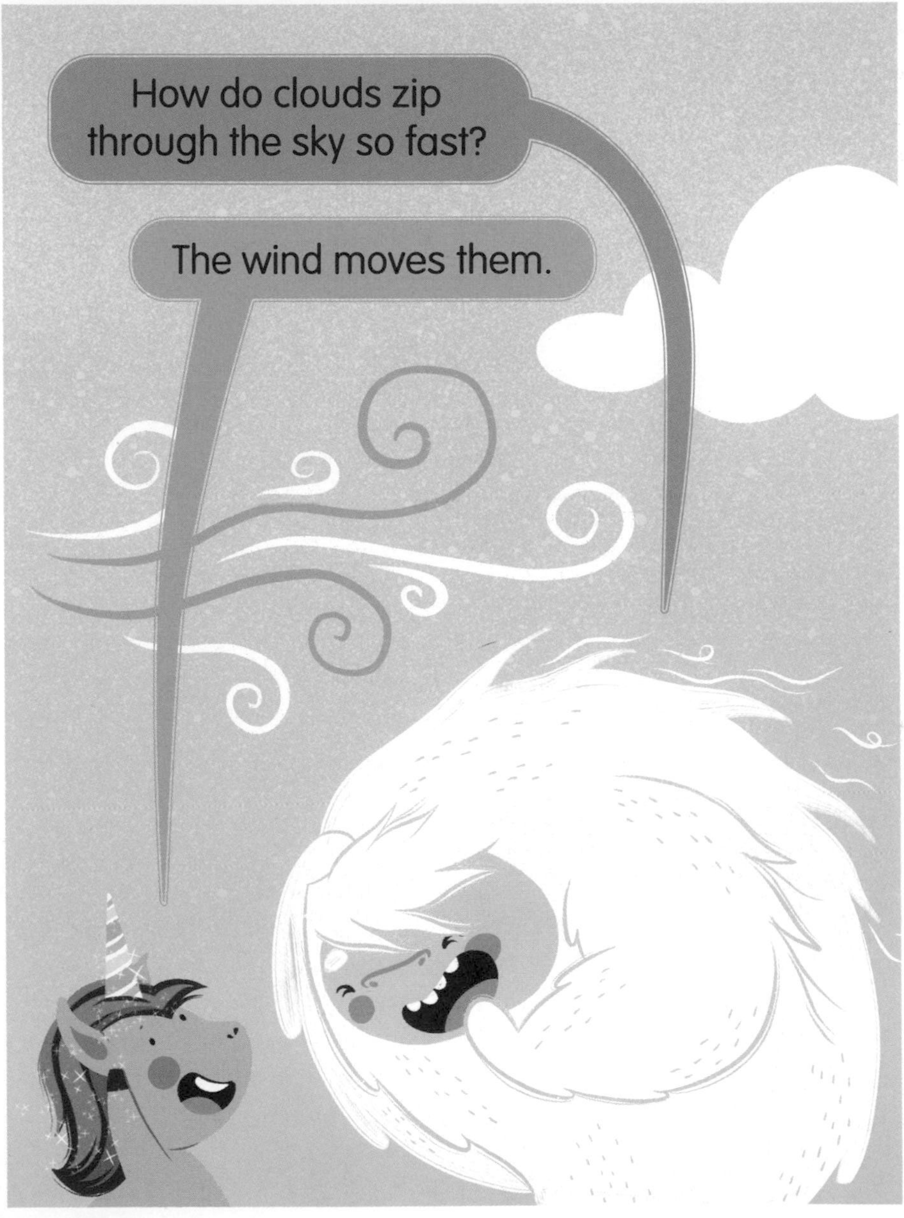
How do clouds zip through the sky so fast?
The wind moves them.

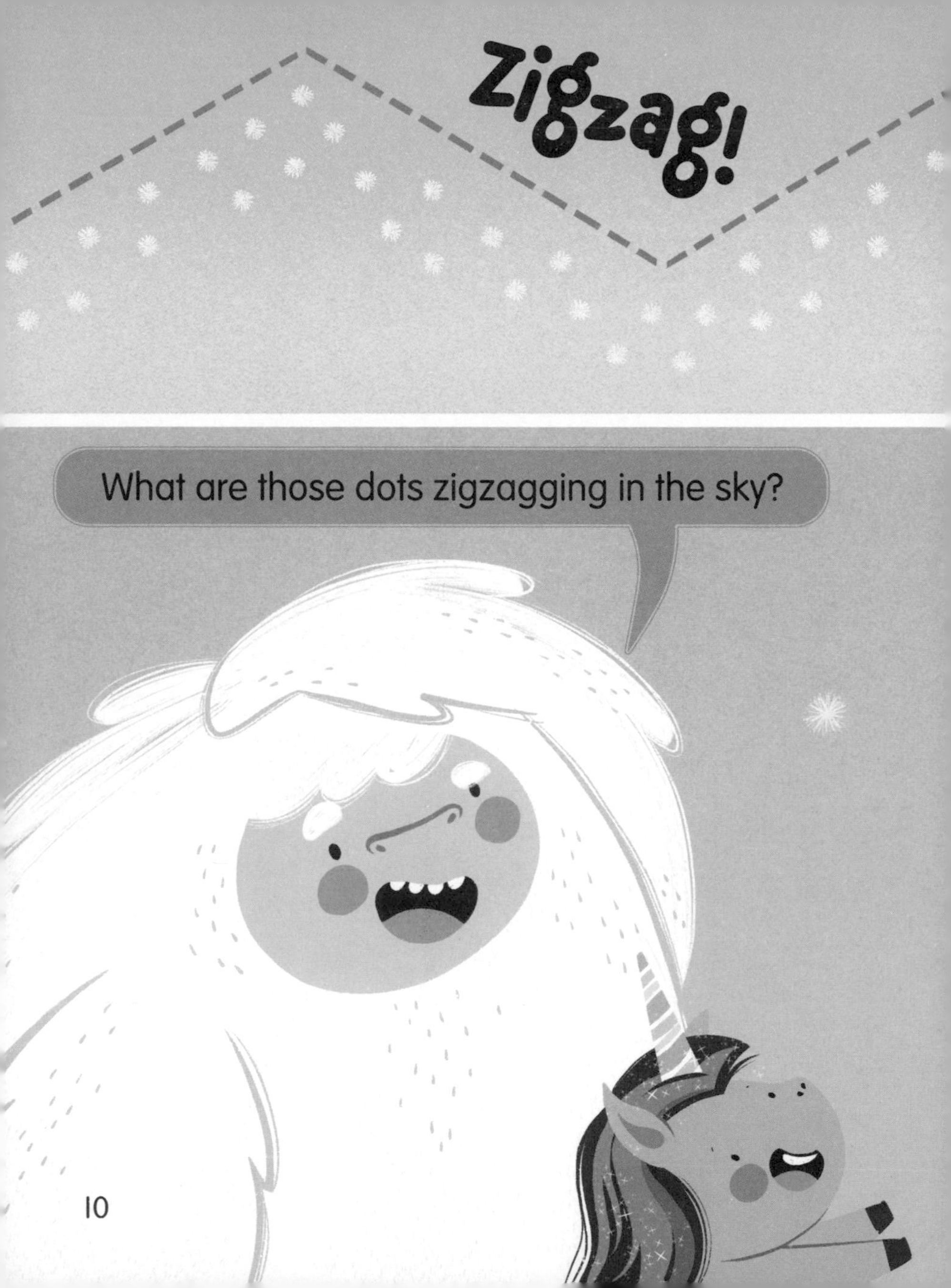
Zigzag!
What are those dots zigzagging in the sky?

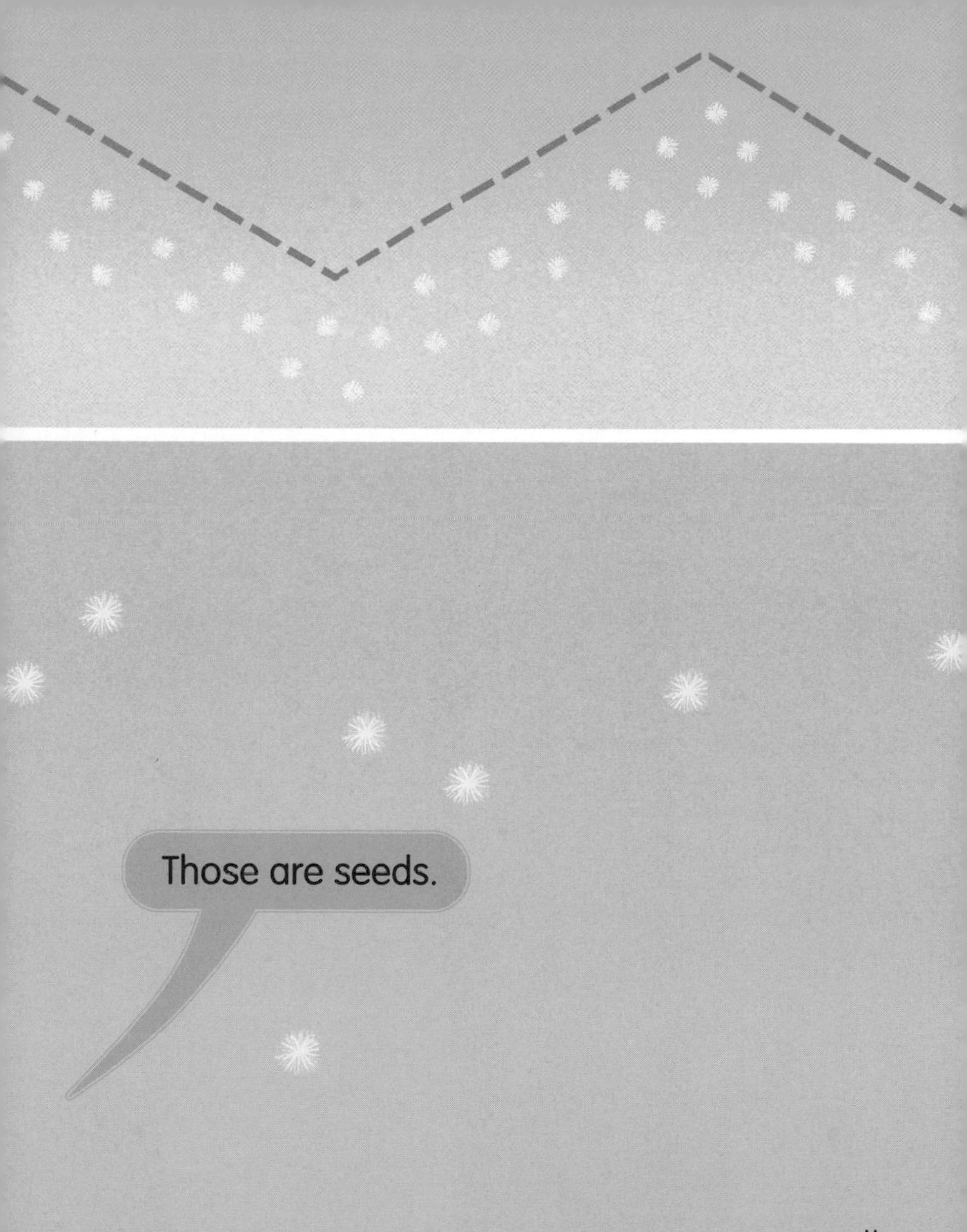
Those are seeds.

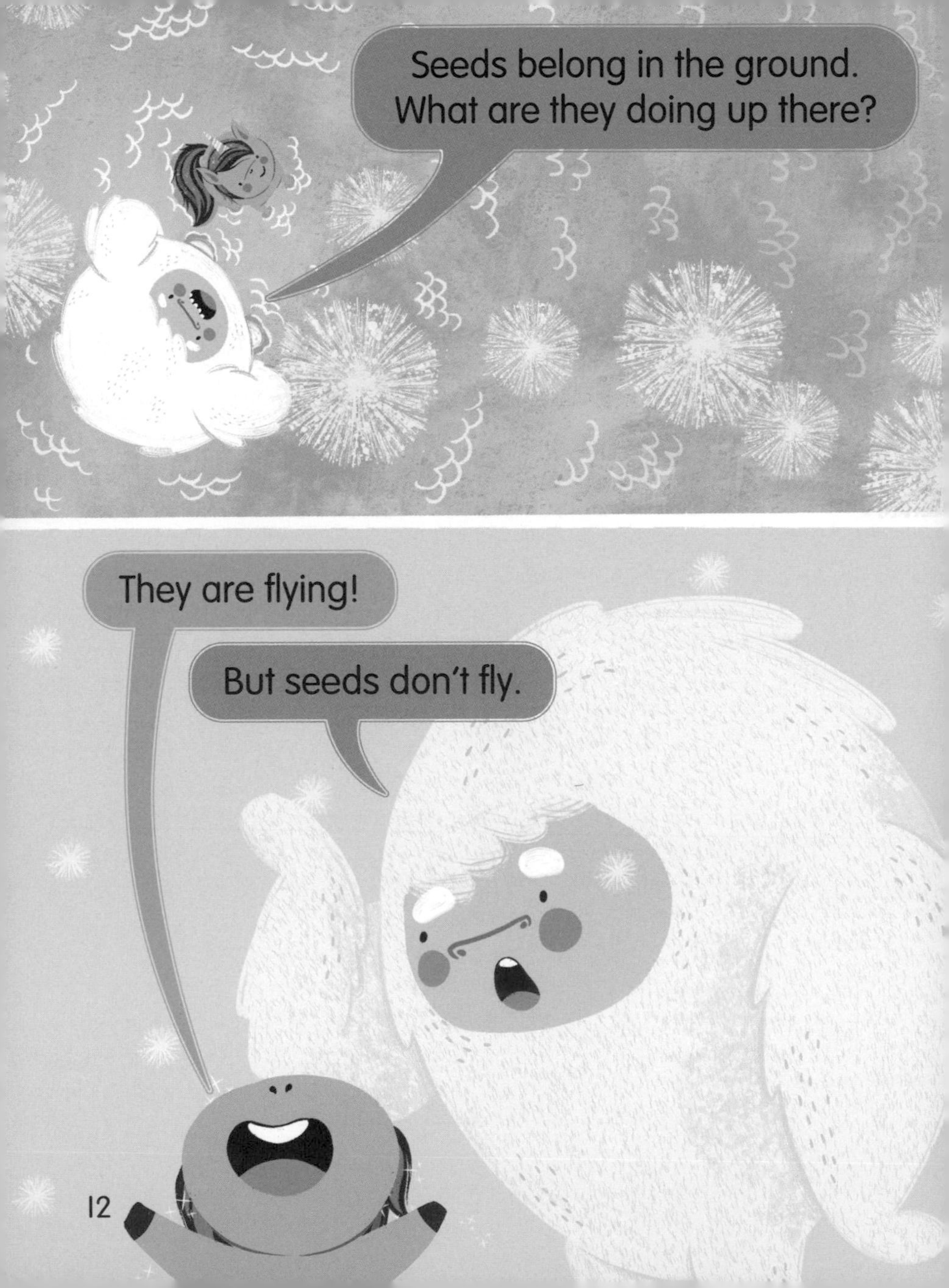
Seeds belong in the ground.
What are they doing up there?
They are flying!
But seeds don't fly.

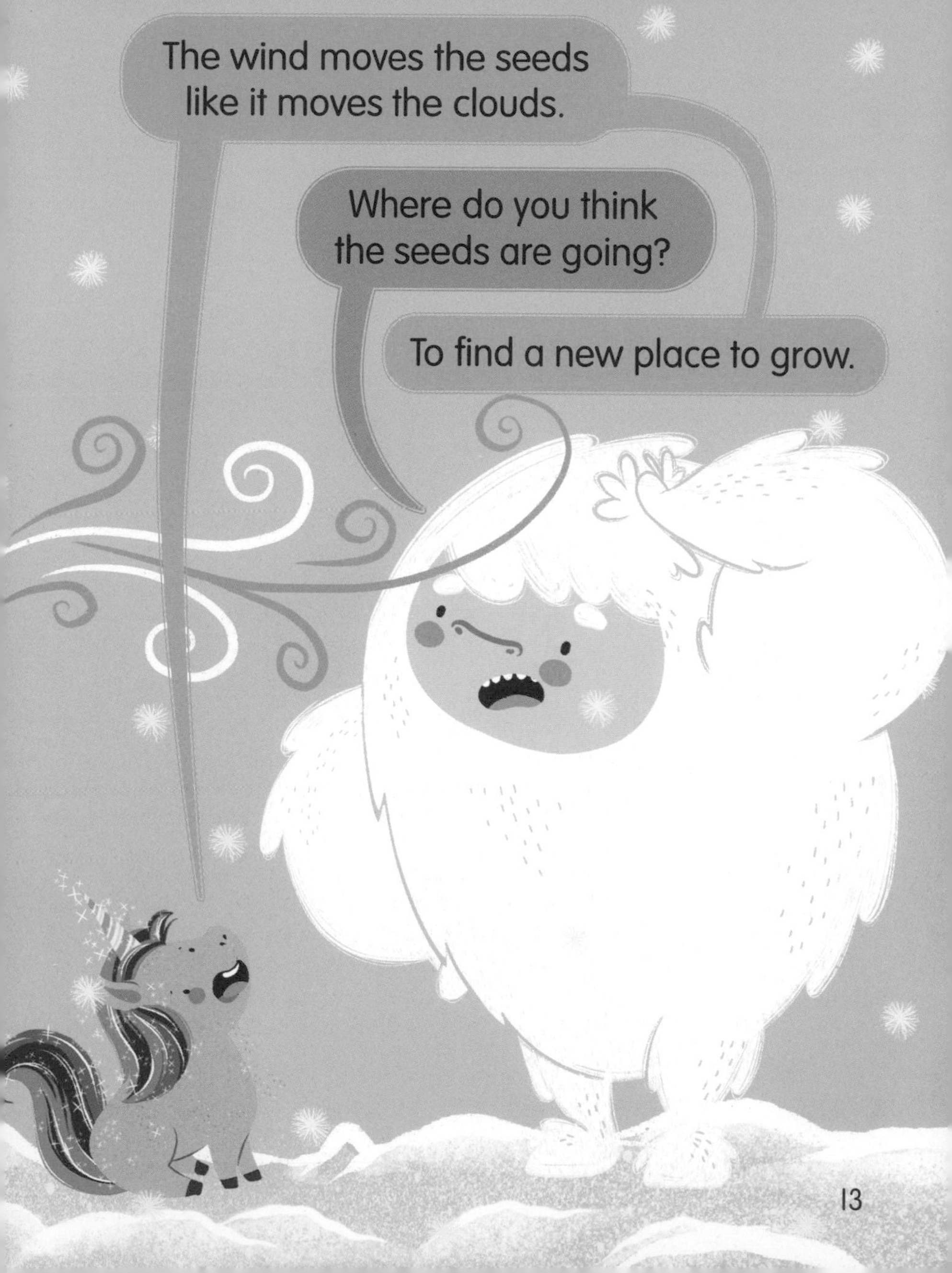
The wind moves the seeds like it moves the clouds.
Where do you think the seeds are going?
To find a new place to grow.

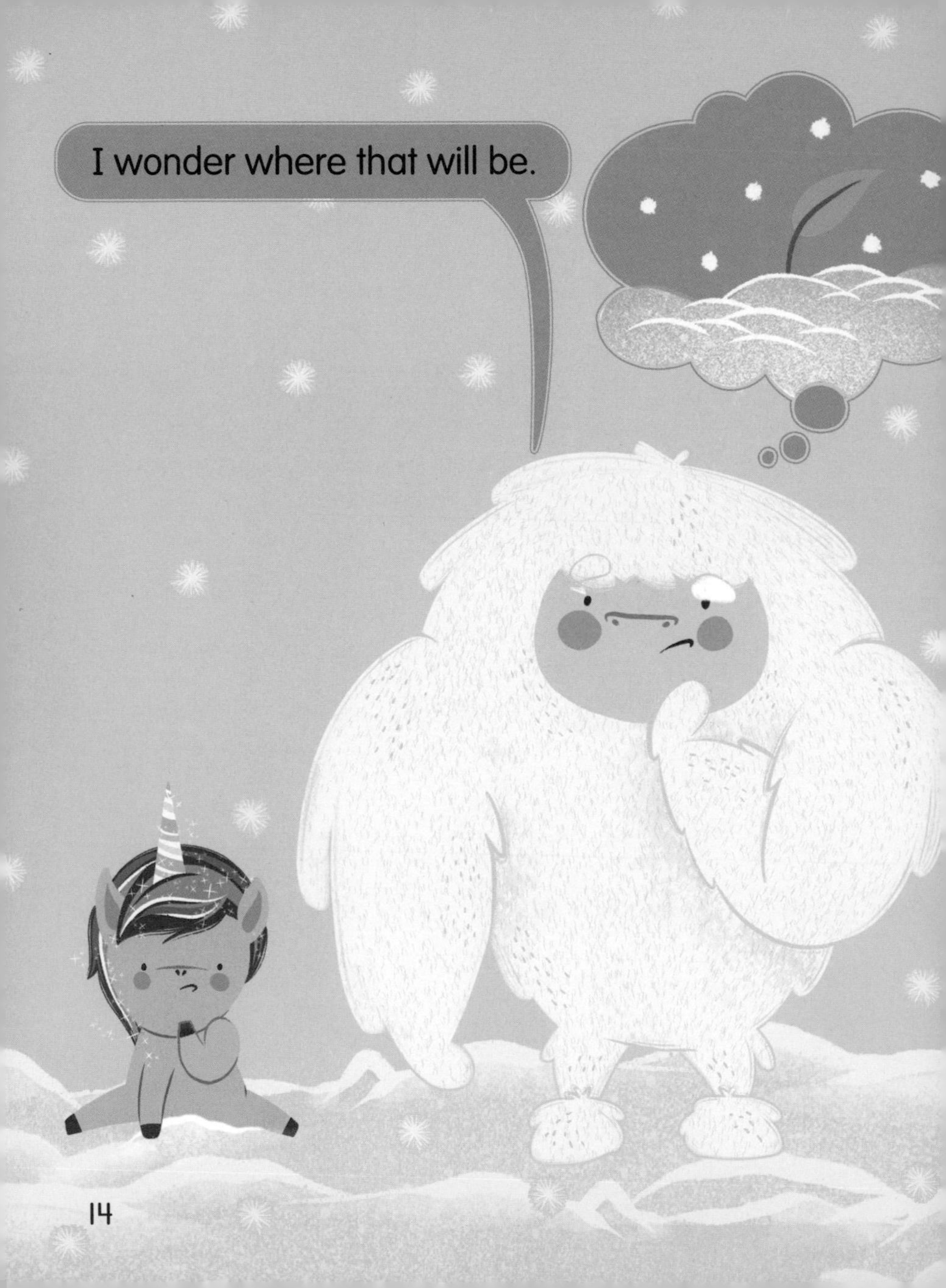
I wonder where that will be.

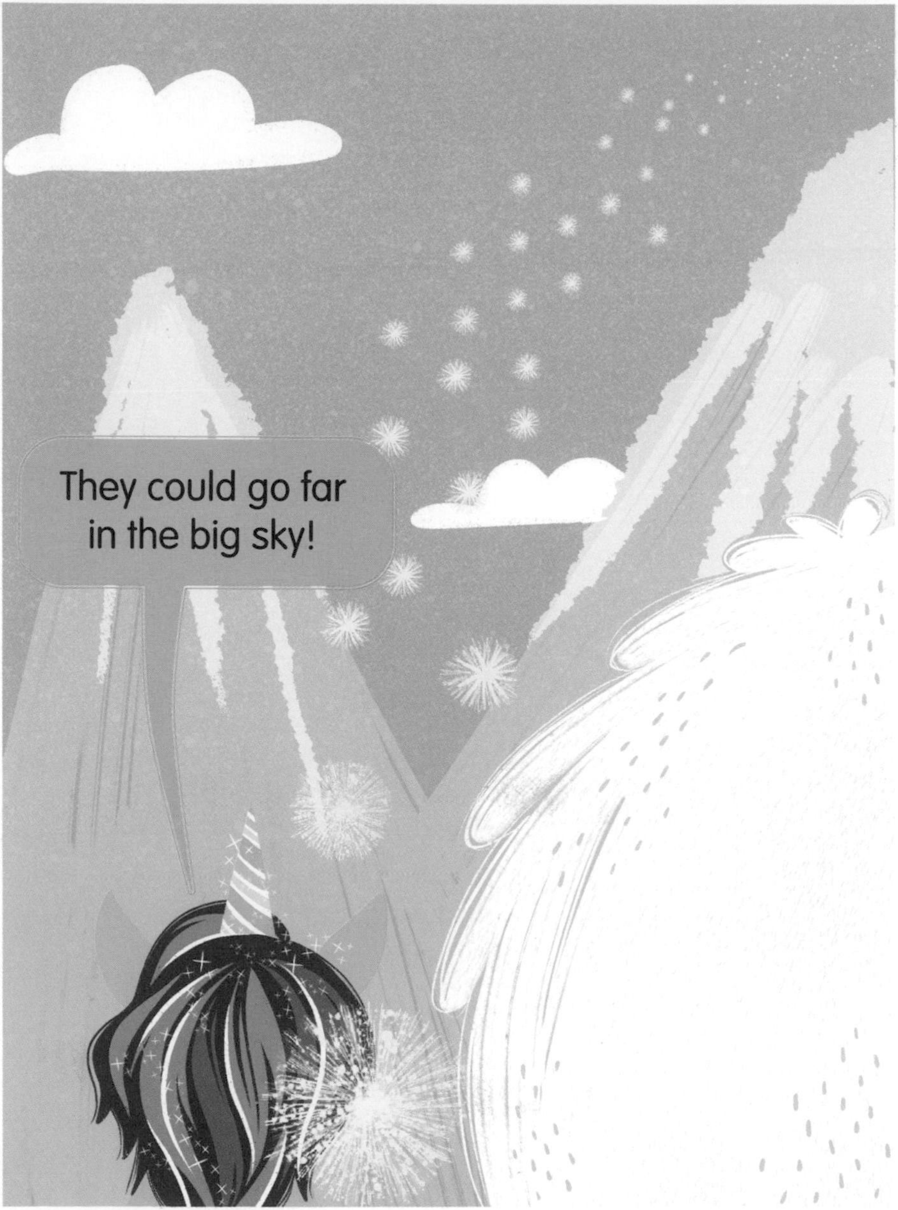
They could go far in the big sky!

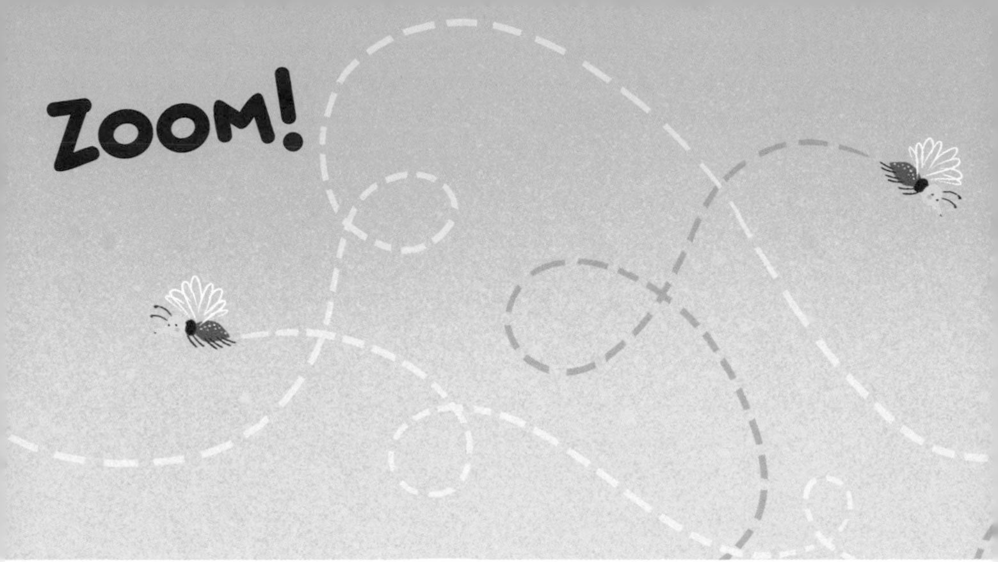
ZOOM!

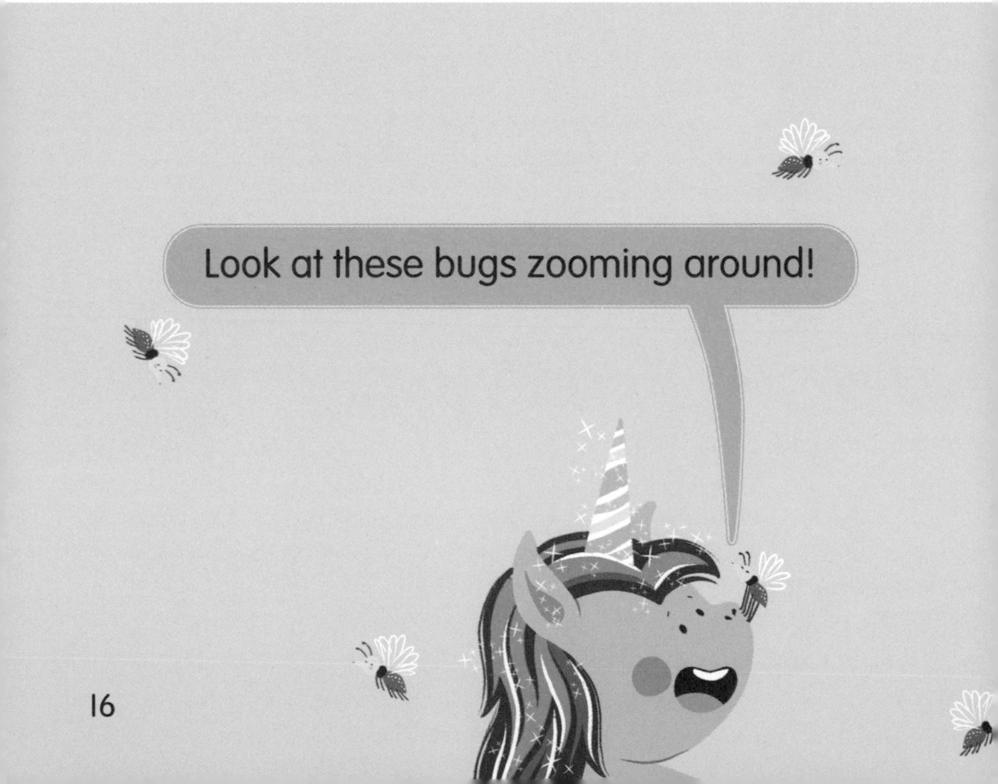
Look at these bugs zooming around!

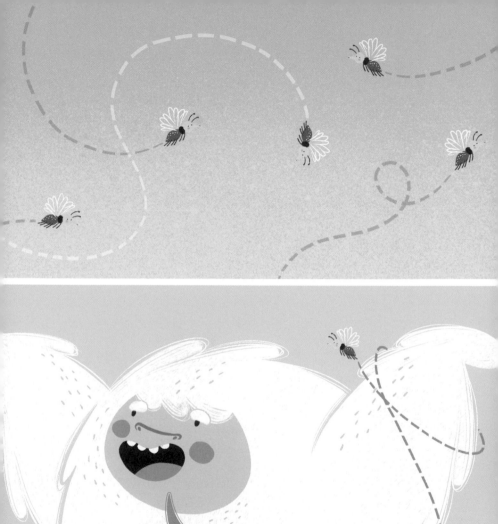

I would like to zoom around.

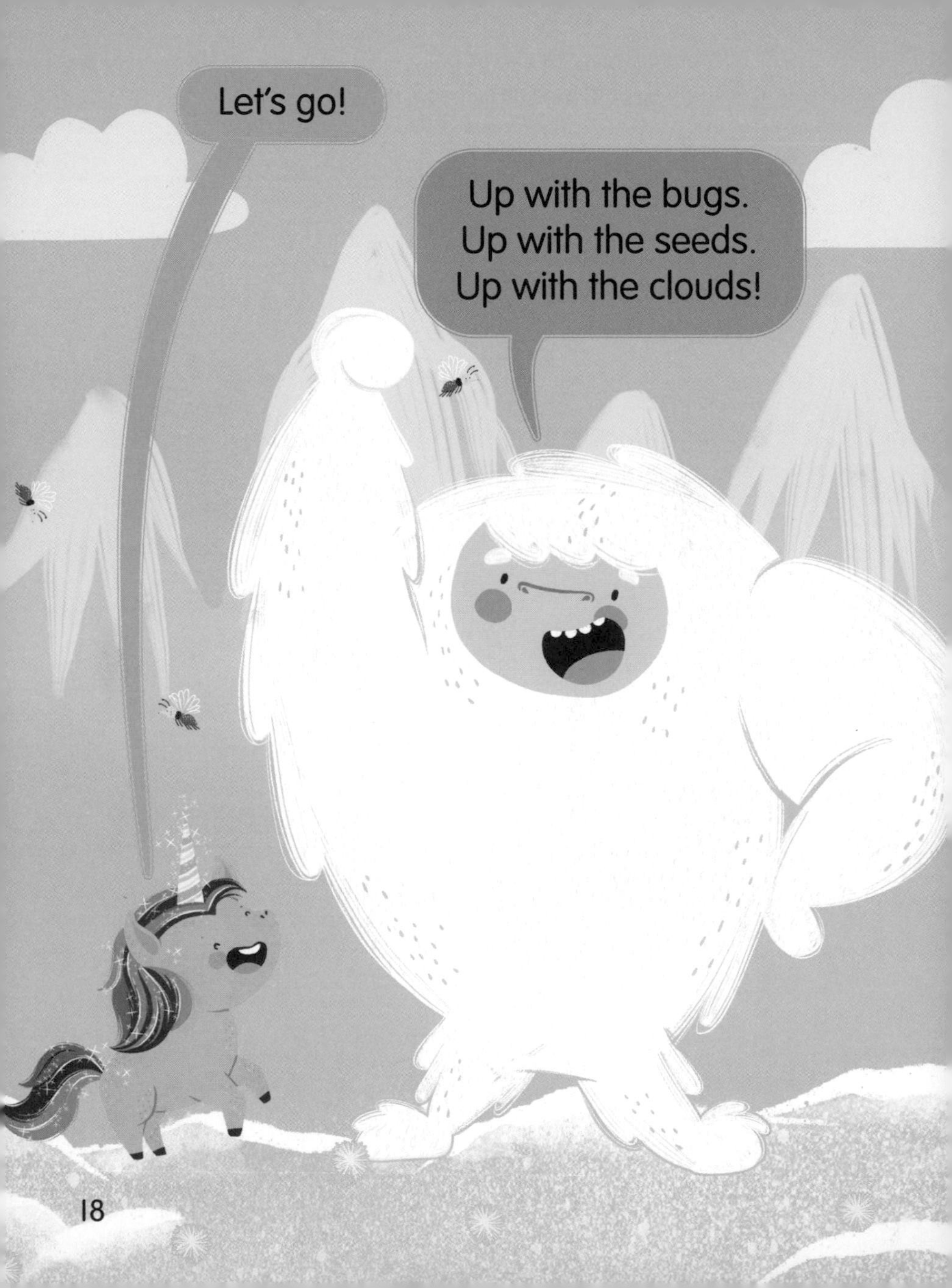
Let's go!
Up with the bugs.
Up with the seeds.
Up with the clouds!

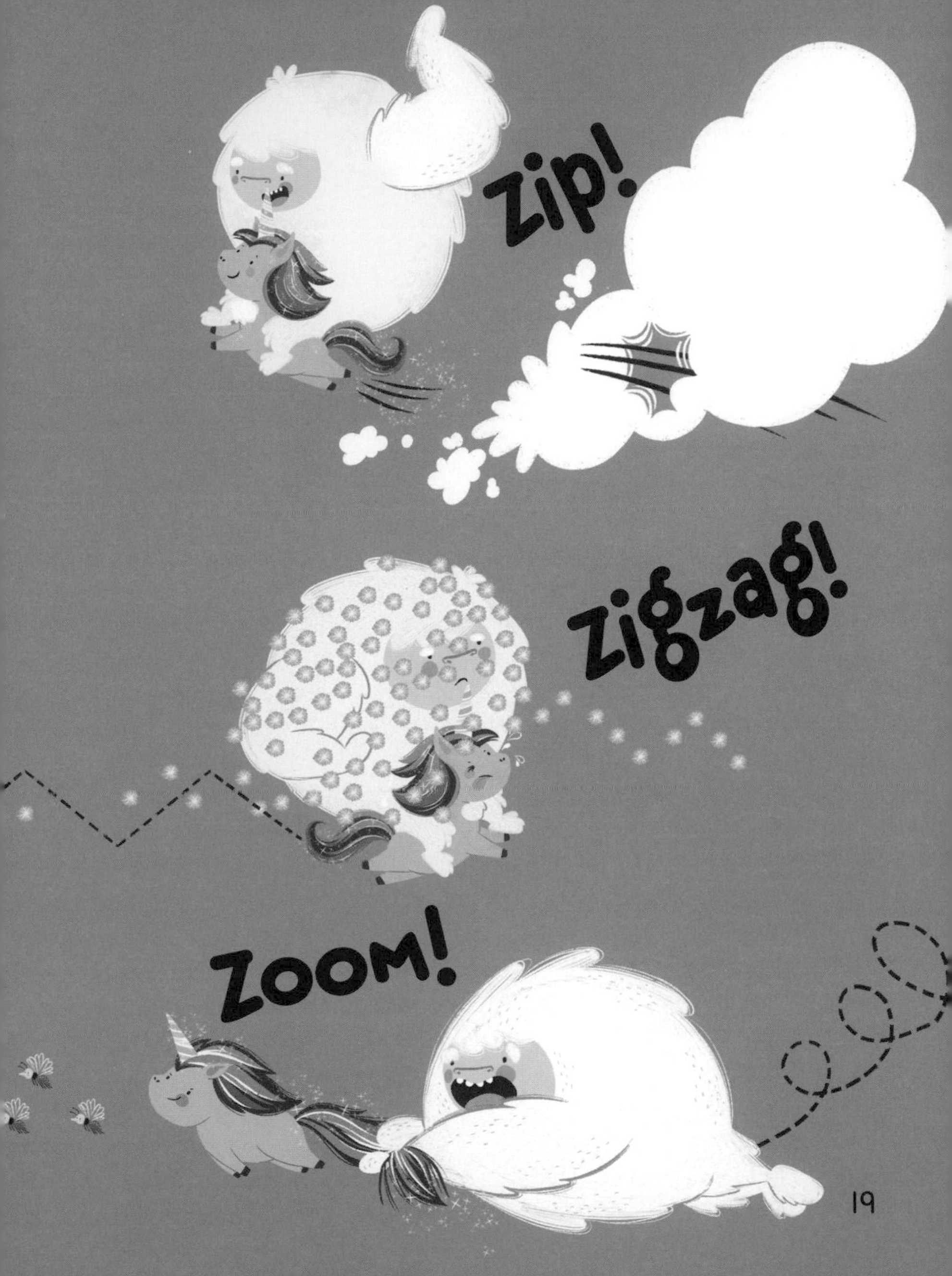
Zip!
Zigzag!
Zoom!

We do not zip like clouds.
We do not zigzag like seeds.
And we do not zoom like bugs.

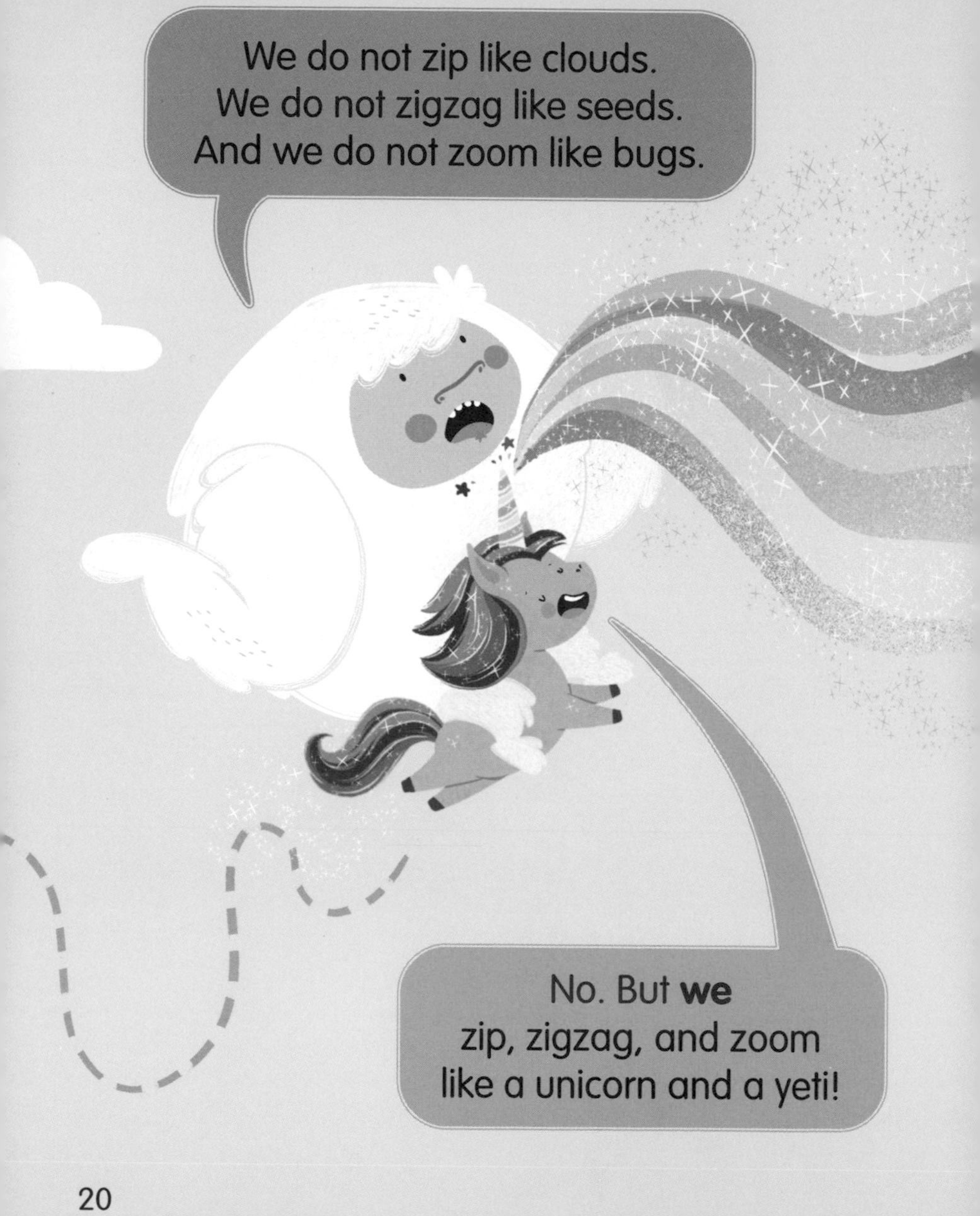

No. But **we**
zip, zigzag, and zoom
like a unicorn and a yeti!

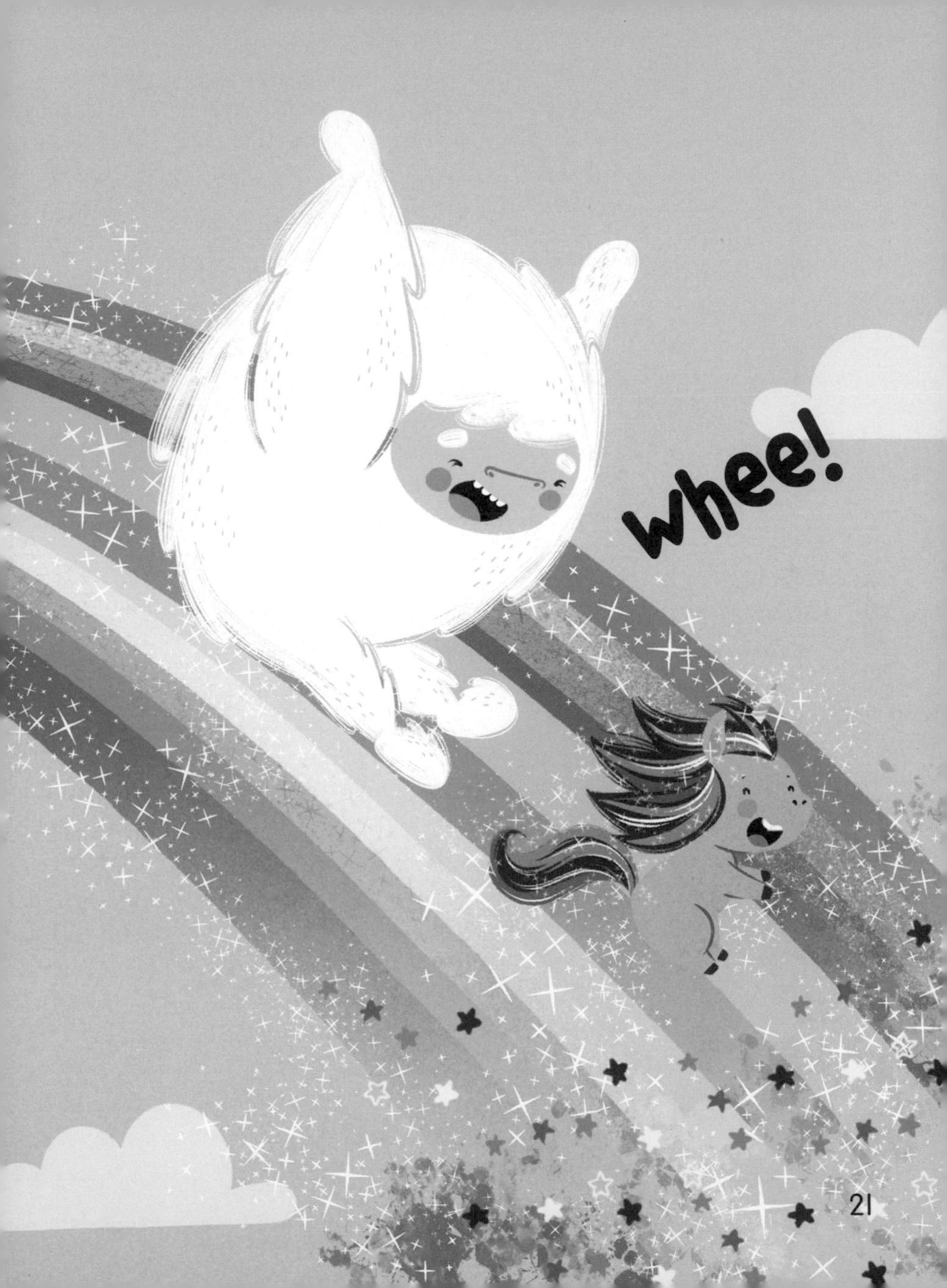
whee!

Copycorn

Unicorn saw Yeti bend to the side.

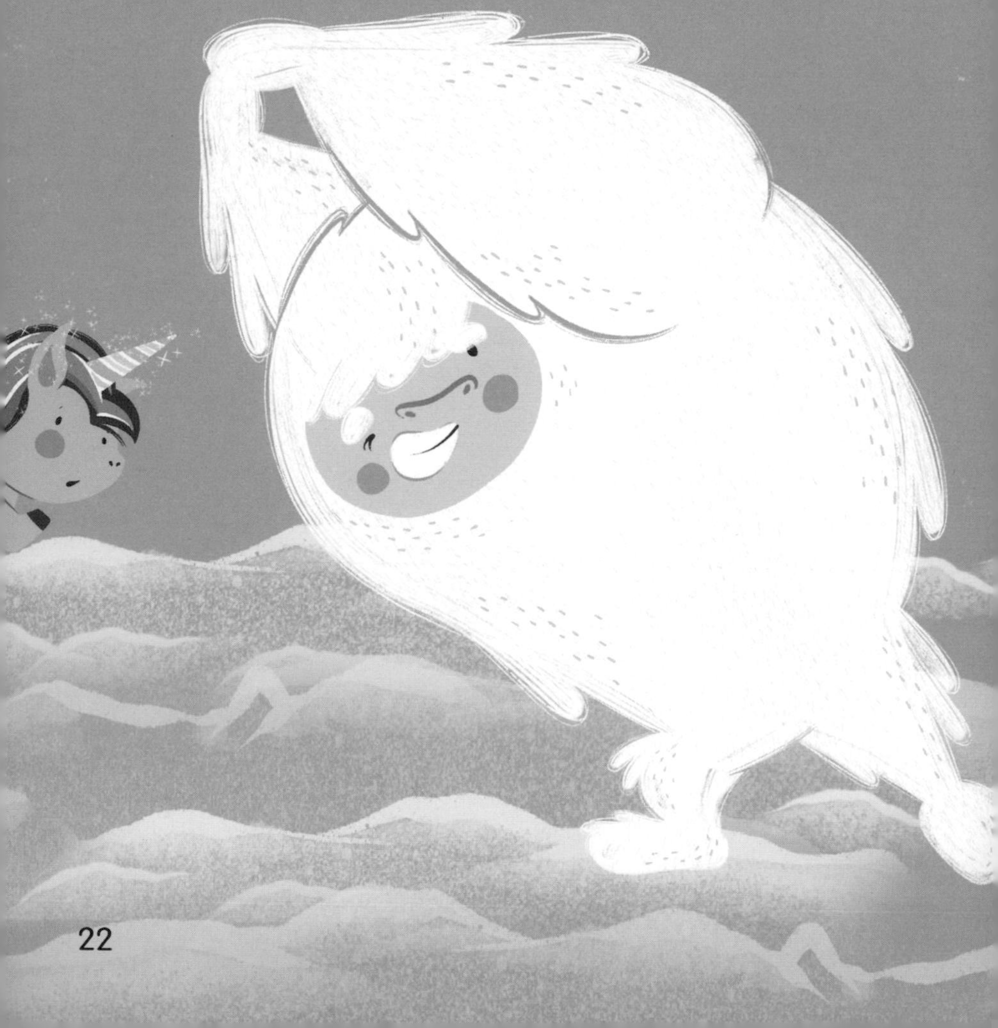

Unicorn saw Yeti leap.

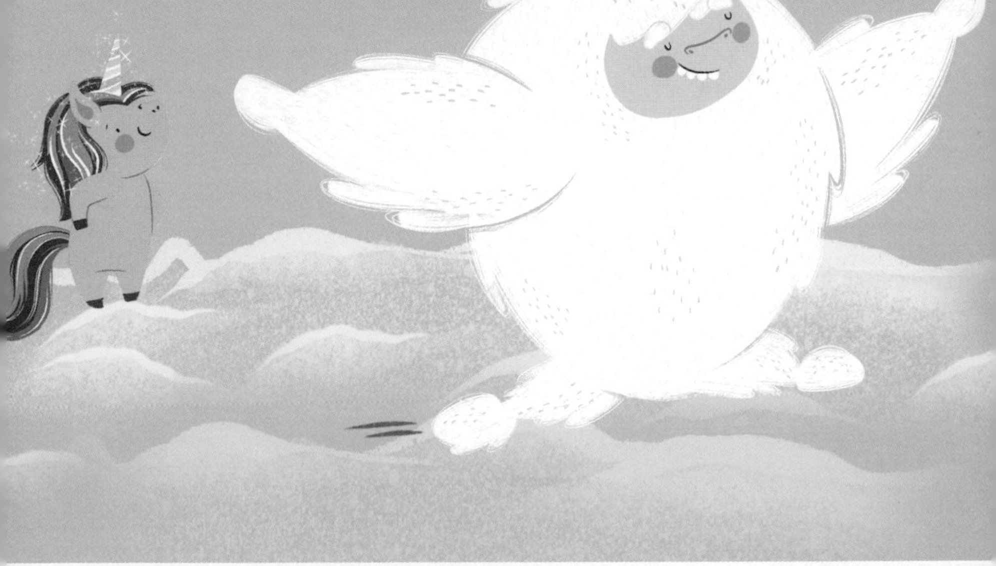

Unicorn leaped.

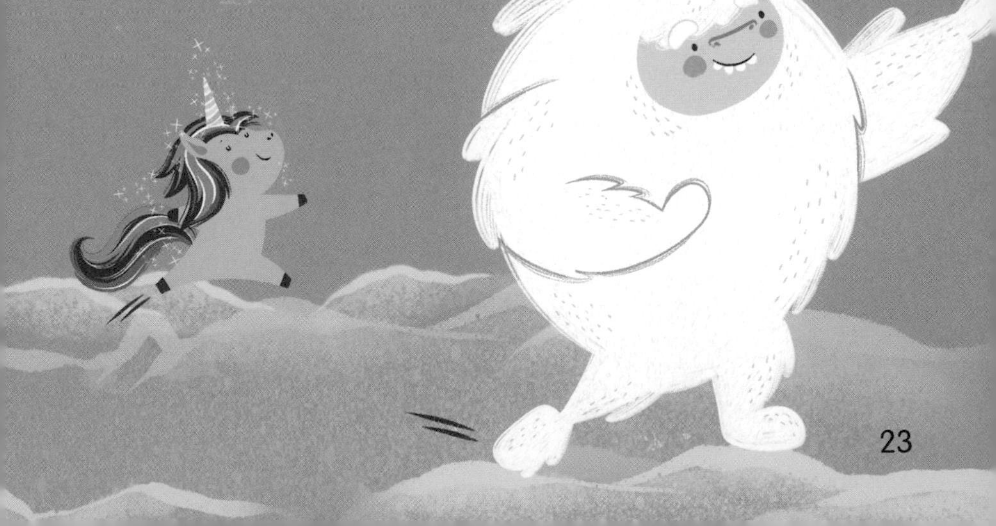

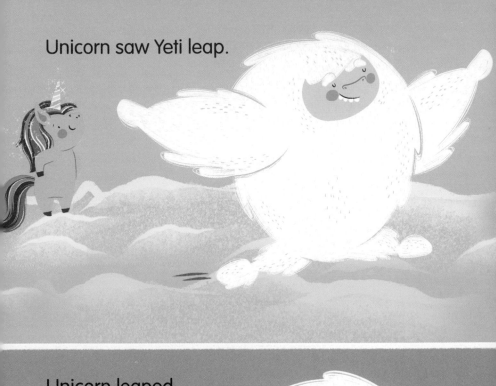

Unicorn saw Yeti twirl.

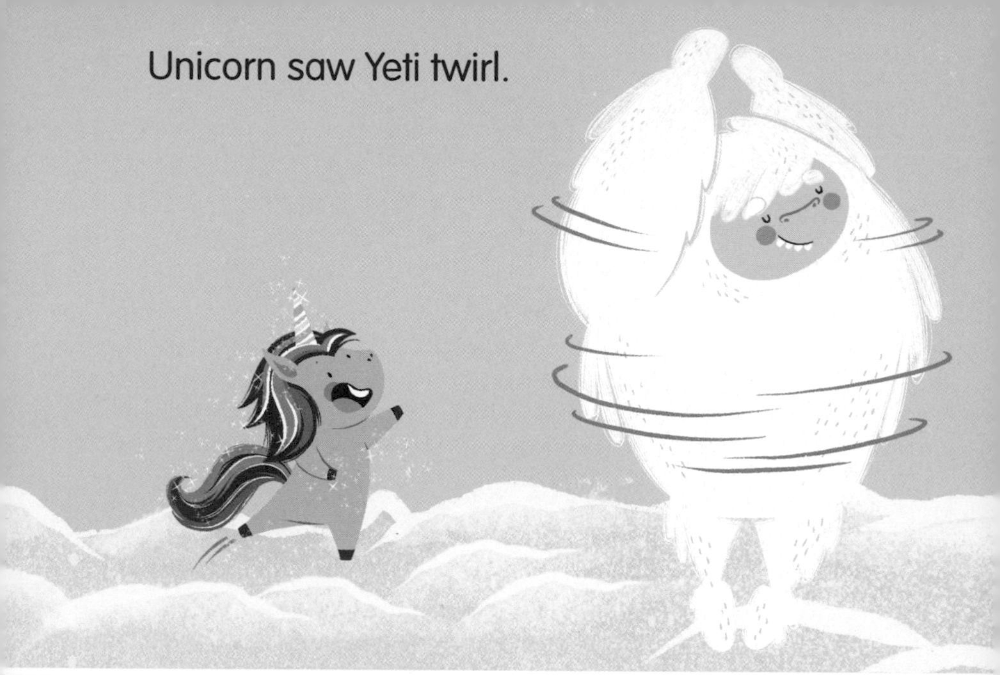

Unicorn twirled.

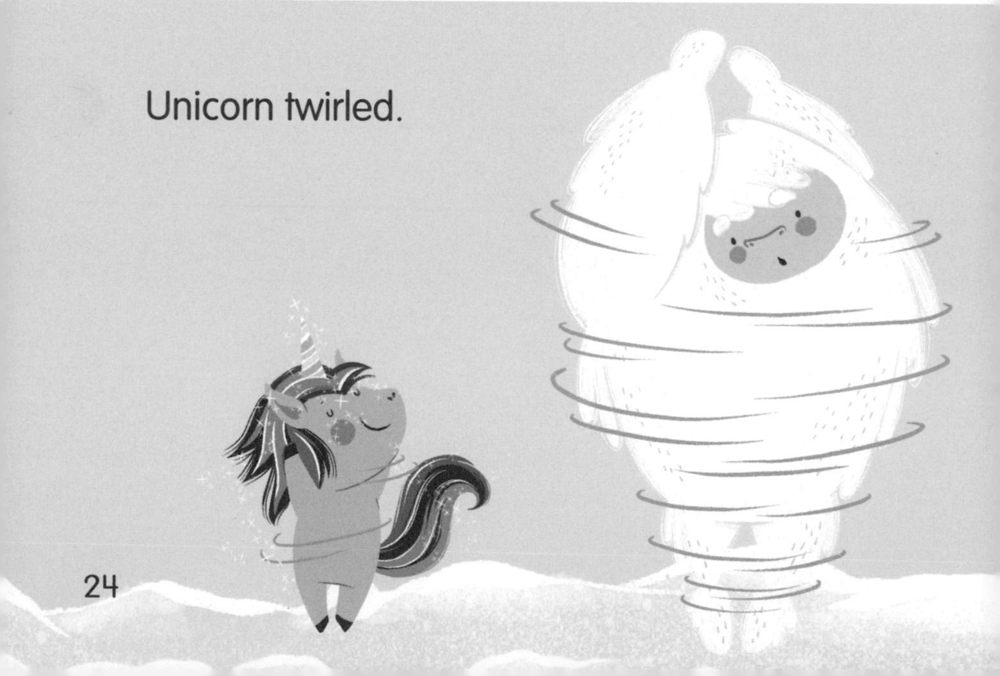

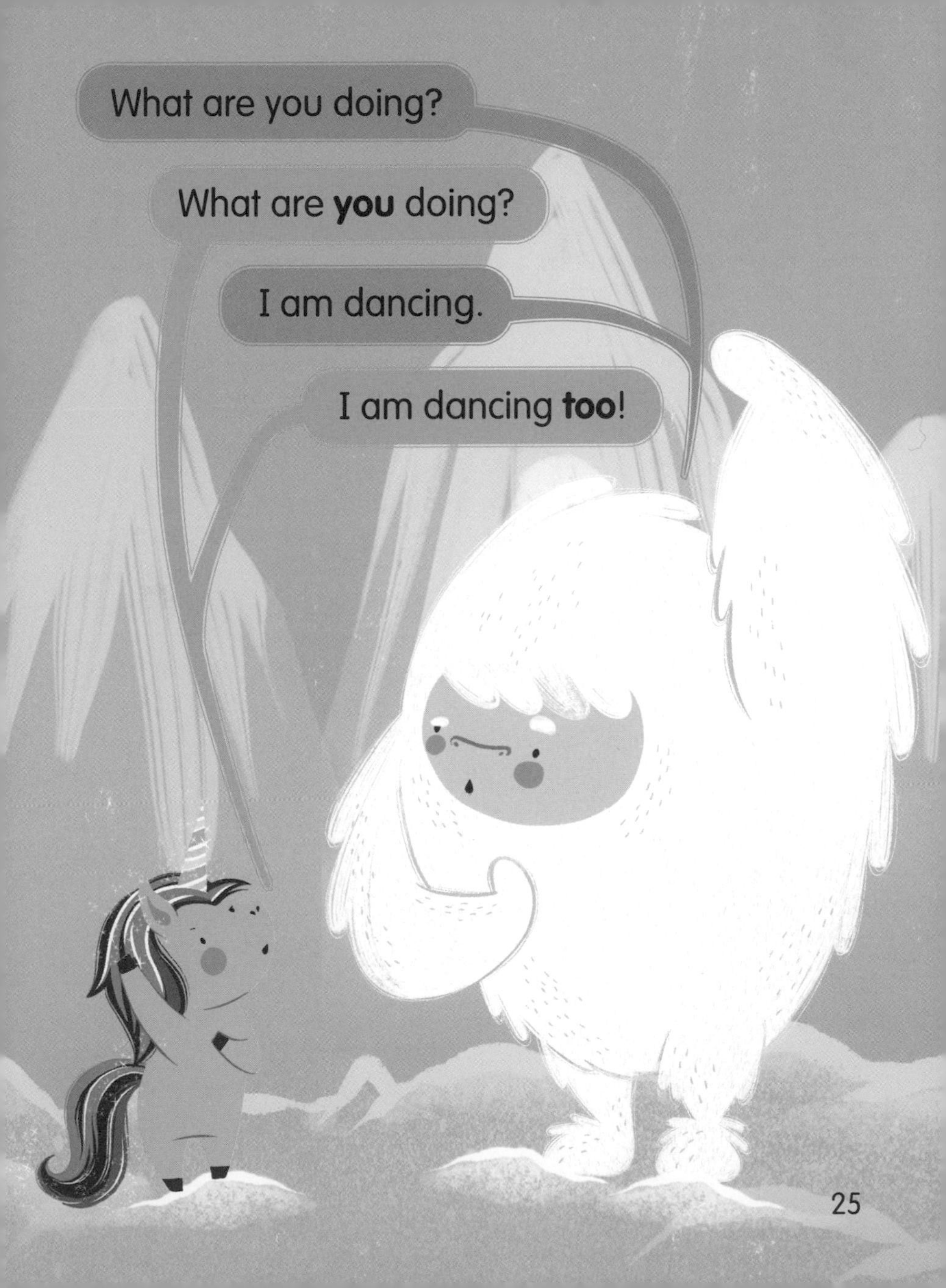
What are you doing?
What are **you** doing?
I am dancing.
I am dancing **too**!

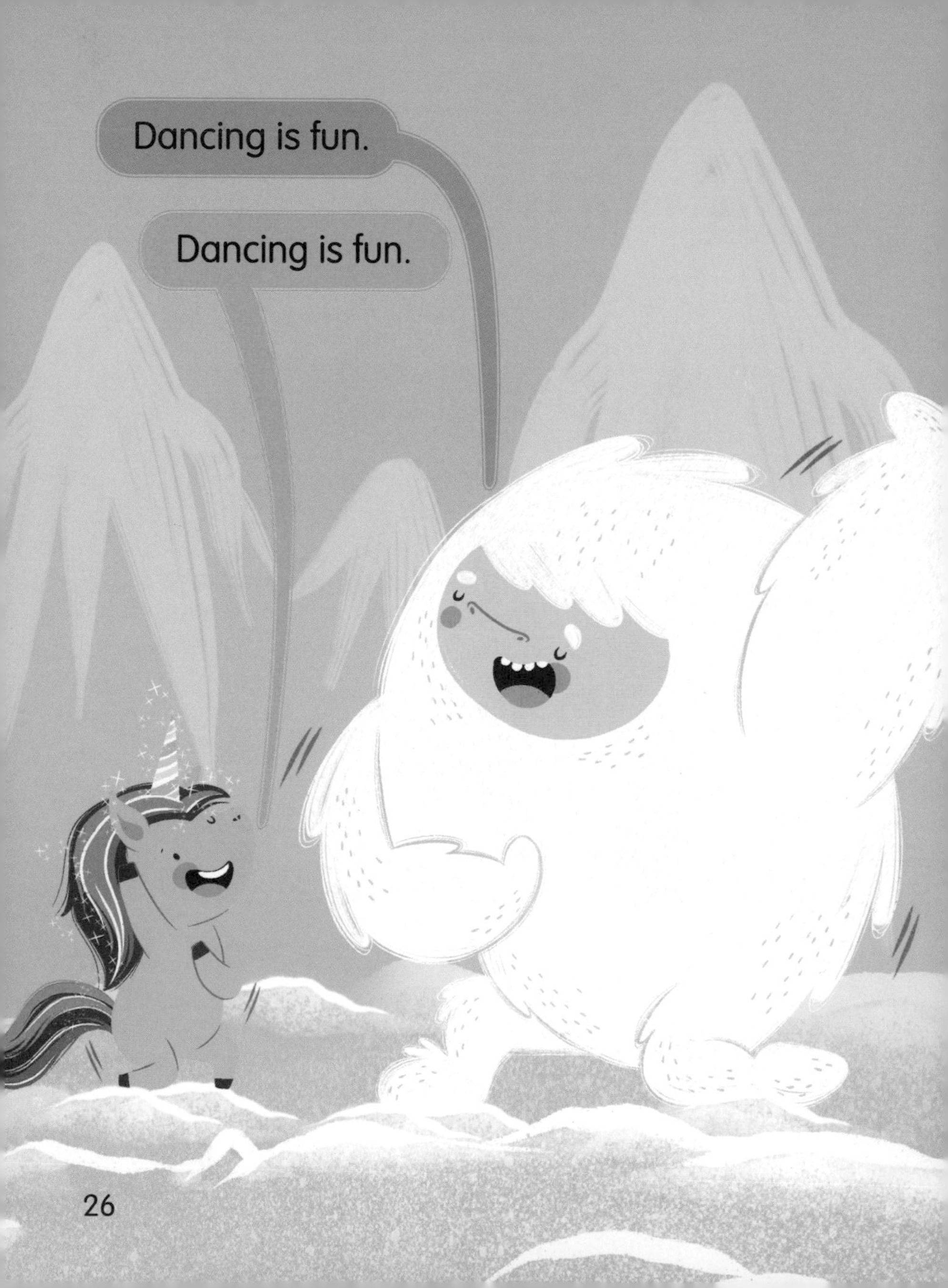
Dancing is fun.
Dancing is fun.

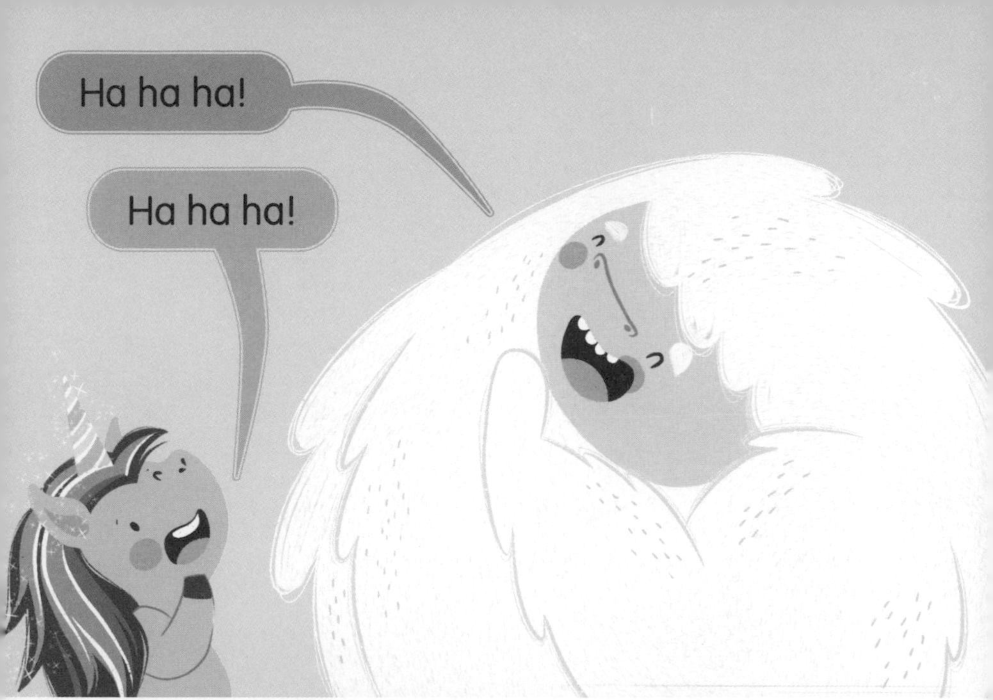
Ha ha ha!
Ha ha ha!

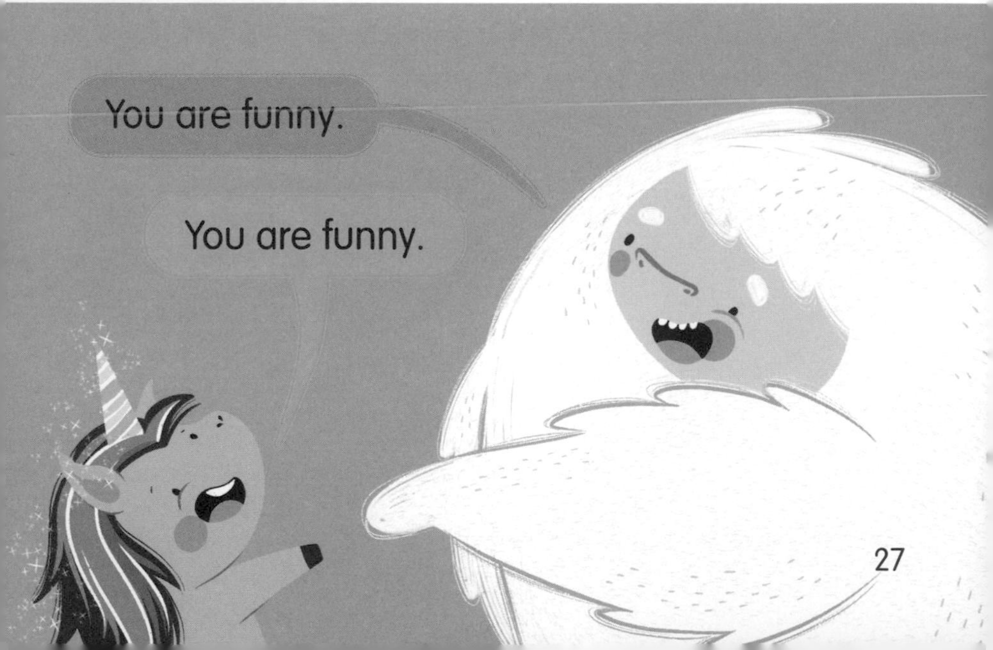
You are funny.
You are funny.

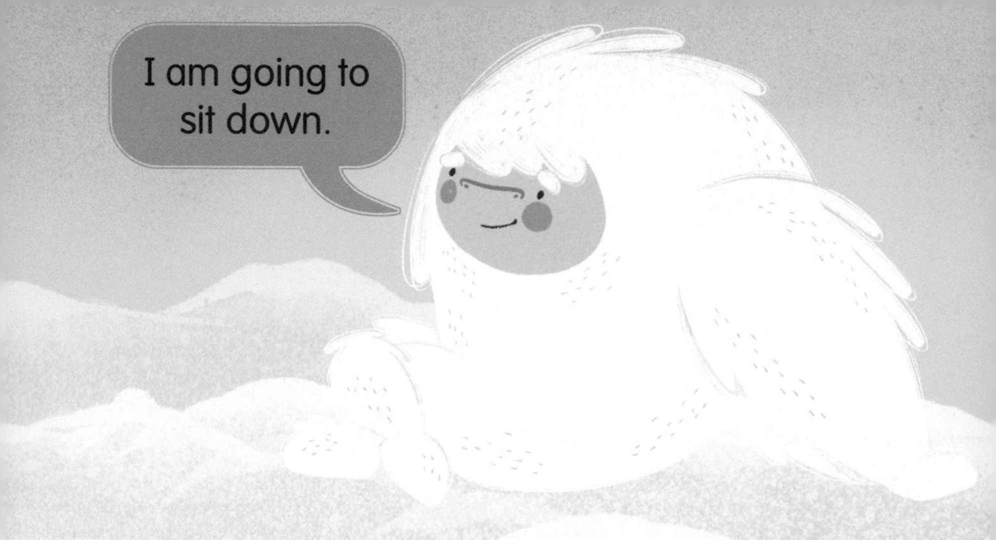
I am going to sit down.

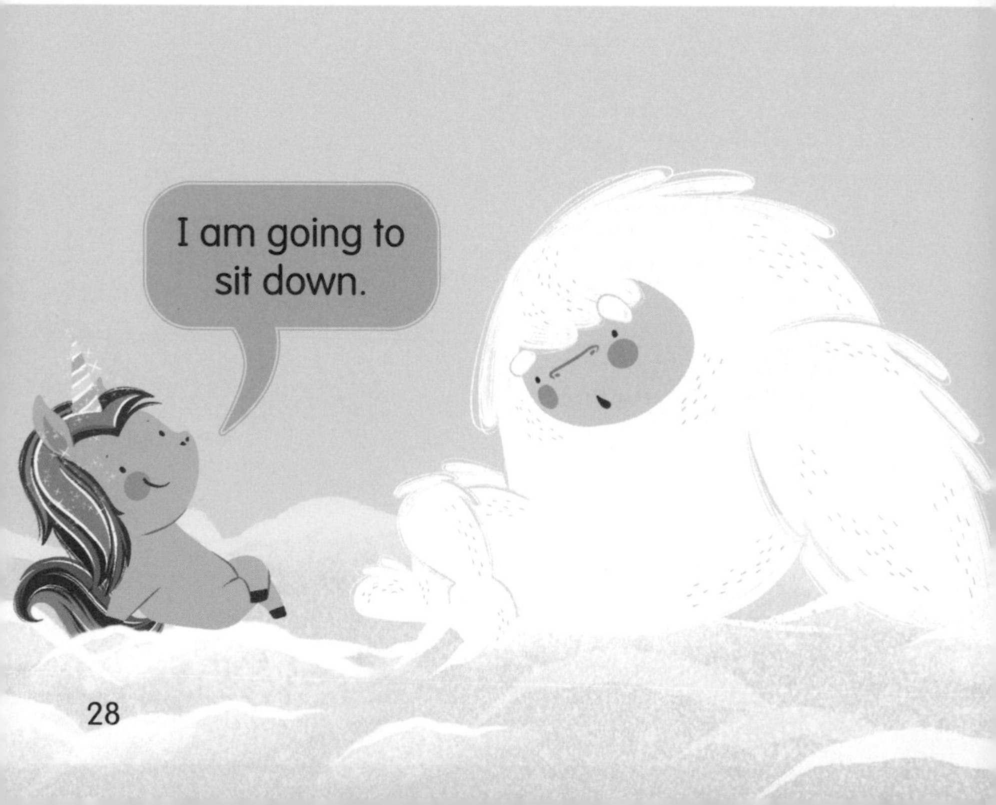
I am going to sit down.

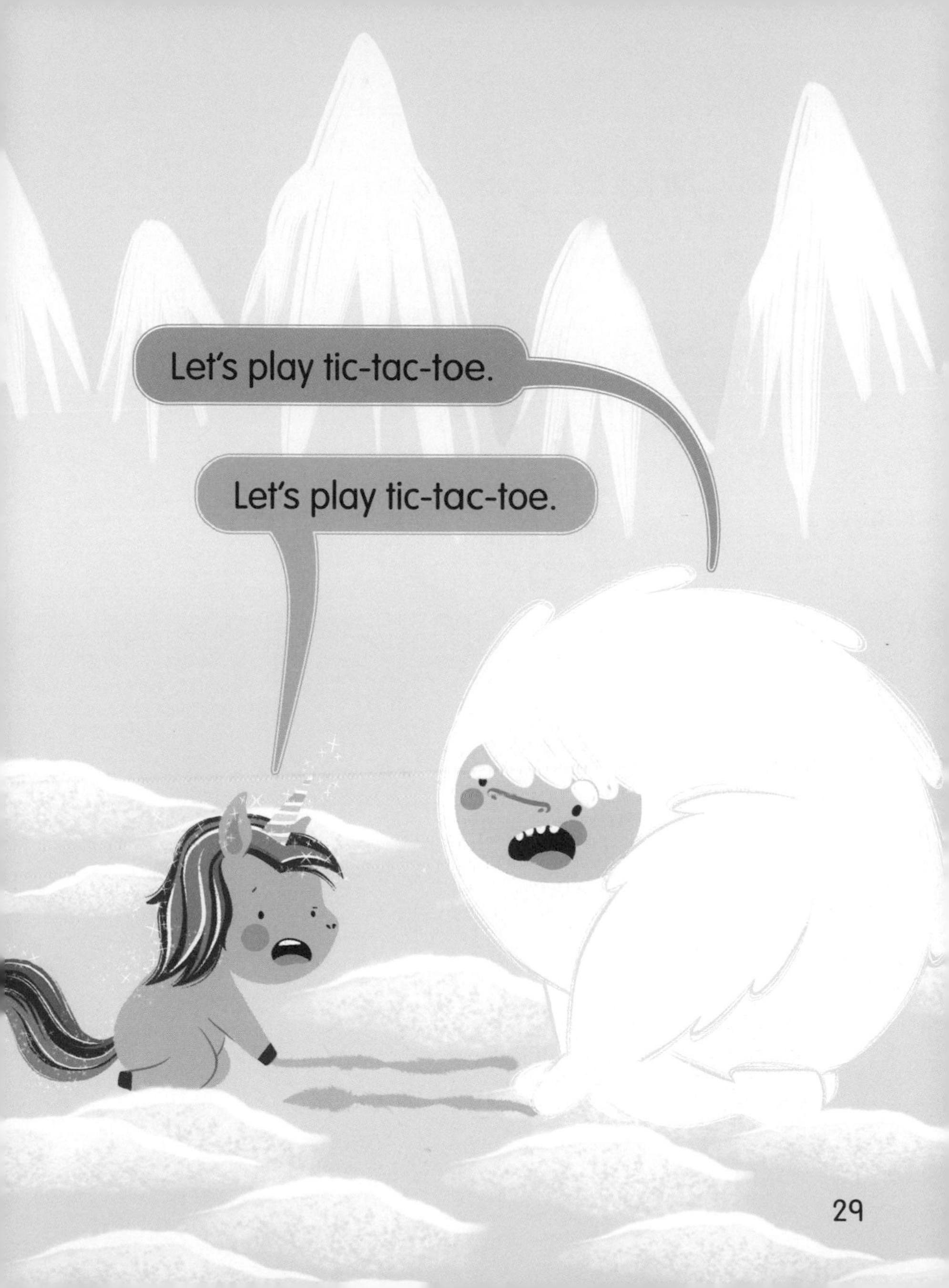
Let's play tic-tac-toe.
Let's play tic-tac-toe.

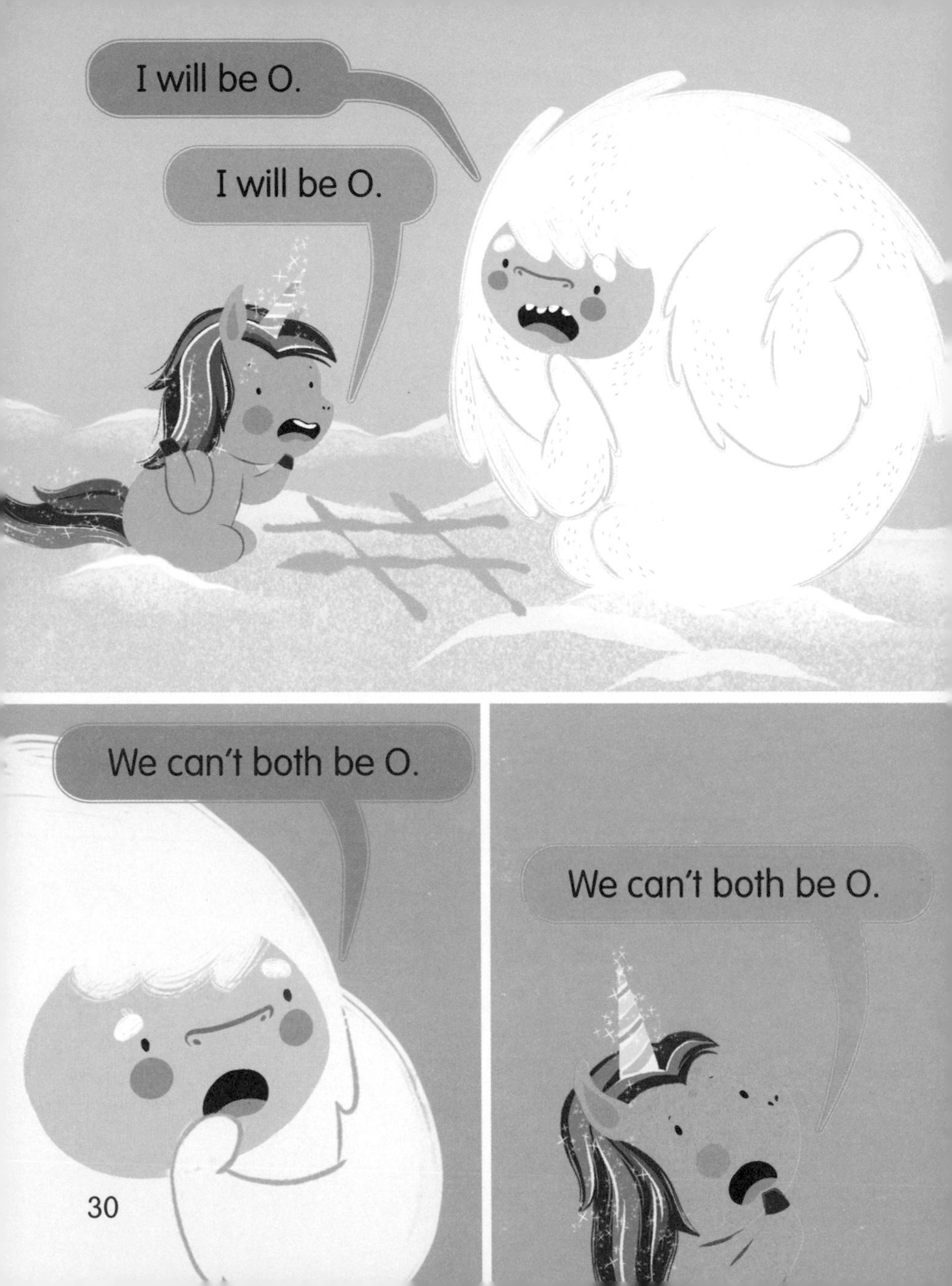
I will be O.
I will be O.
We can't both be O.
We can't both be O.

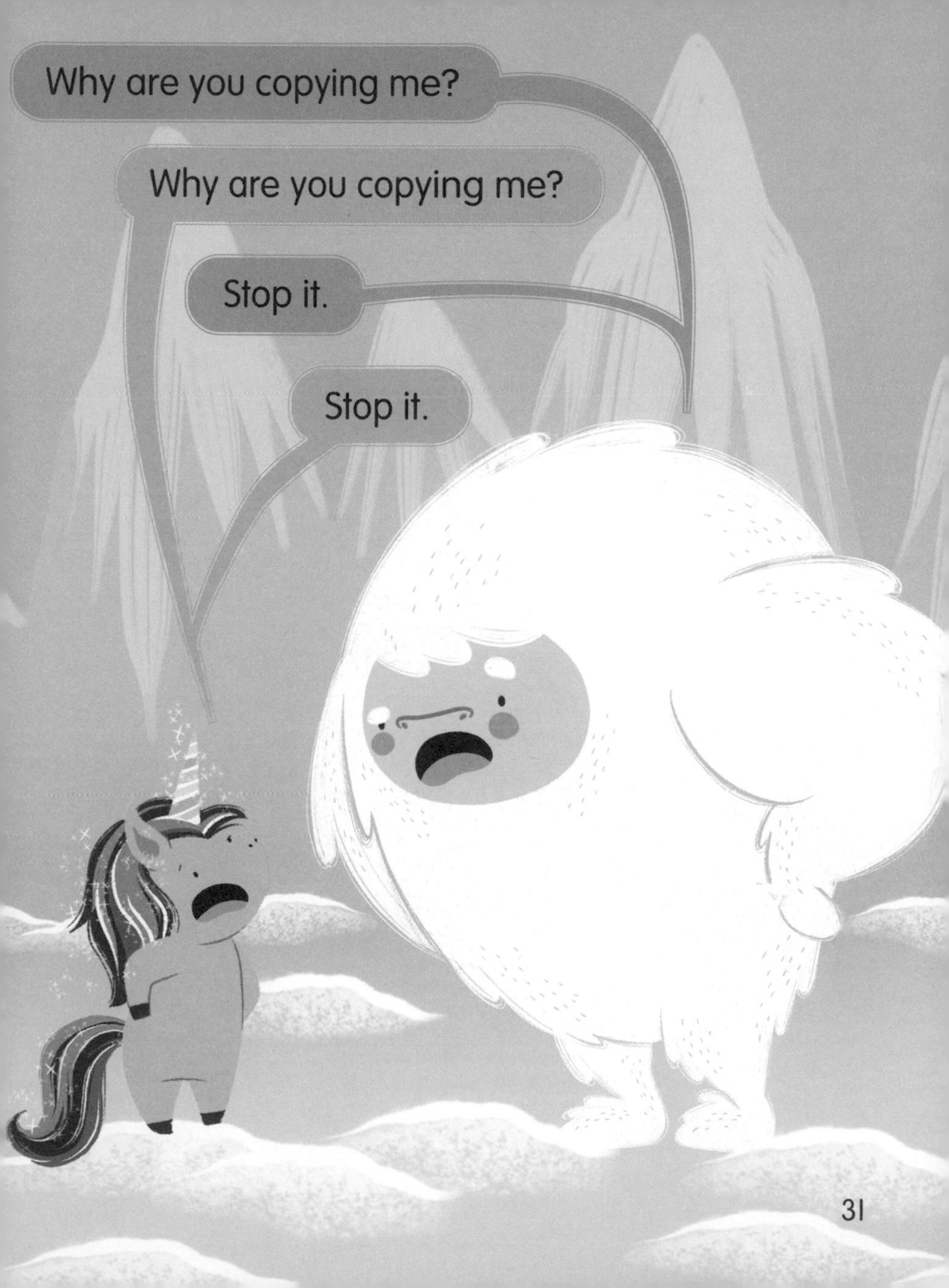
Why are you copying me?
Why are you copying me?
Stop it.
Stop it.

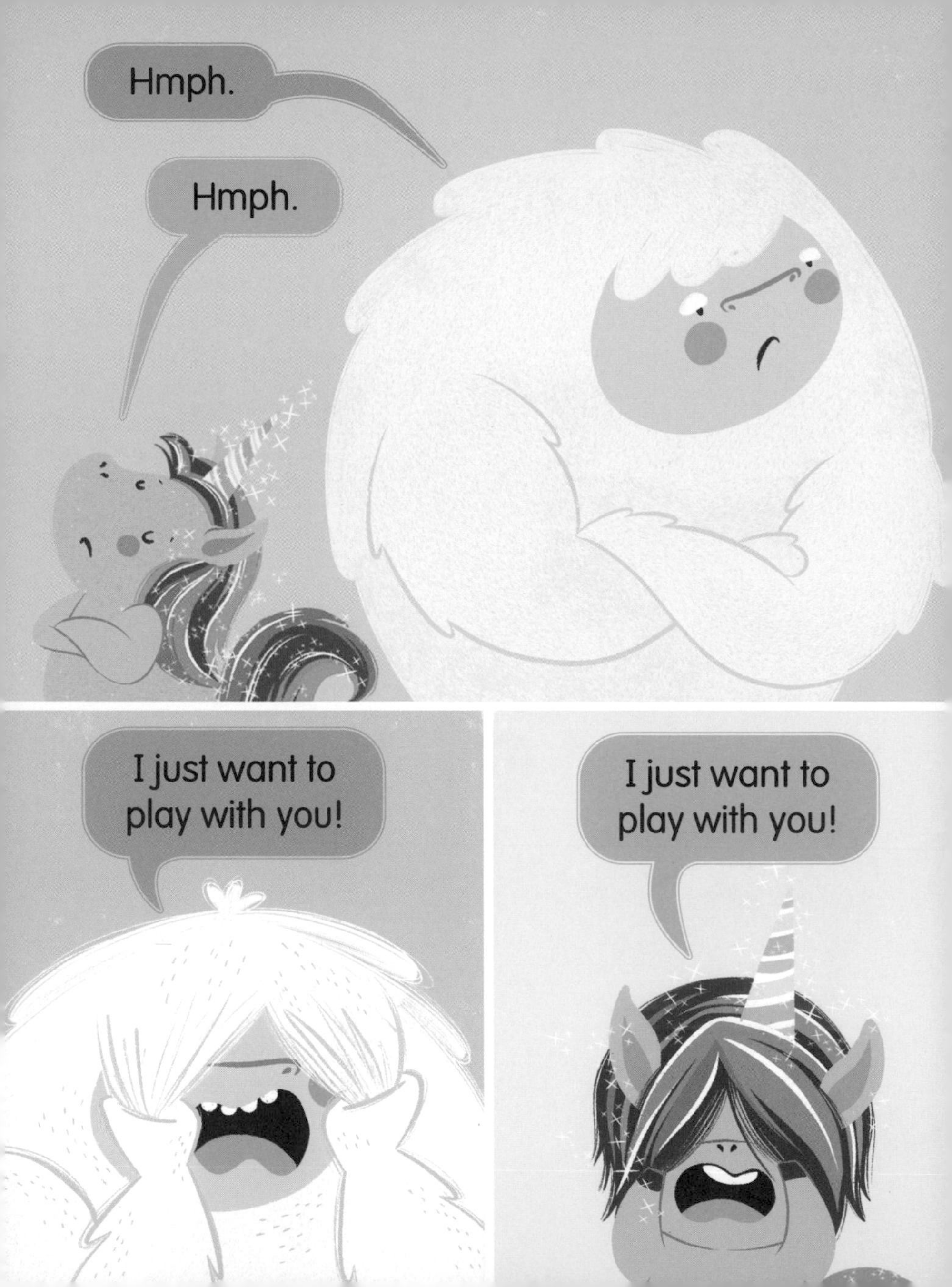
Hmph.
Hmph.
I just want to play with you!
I just want to play with you!

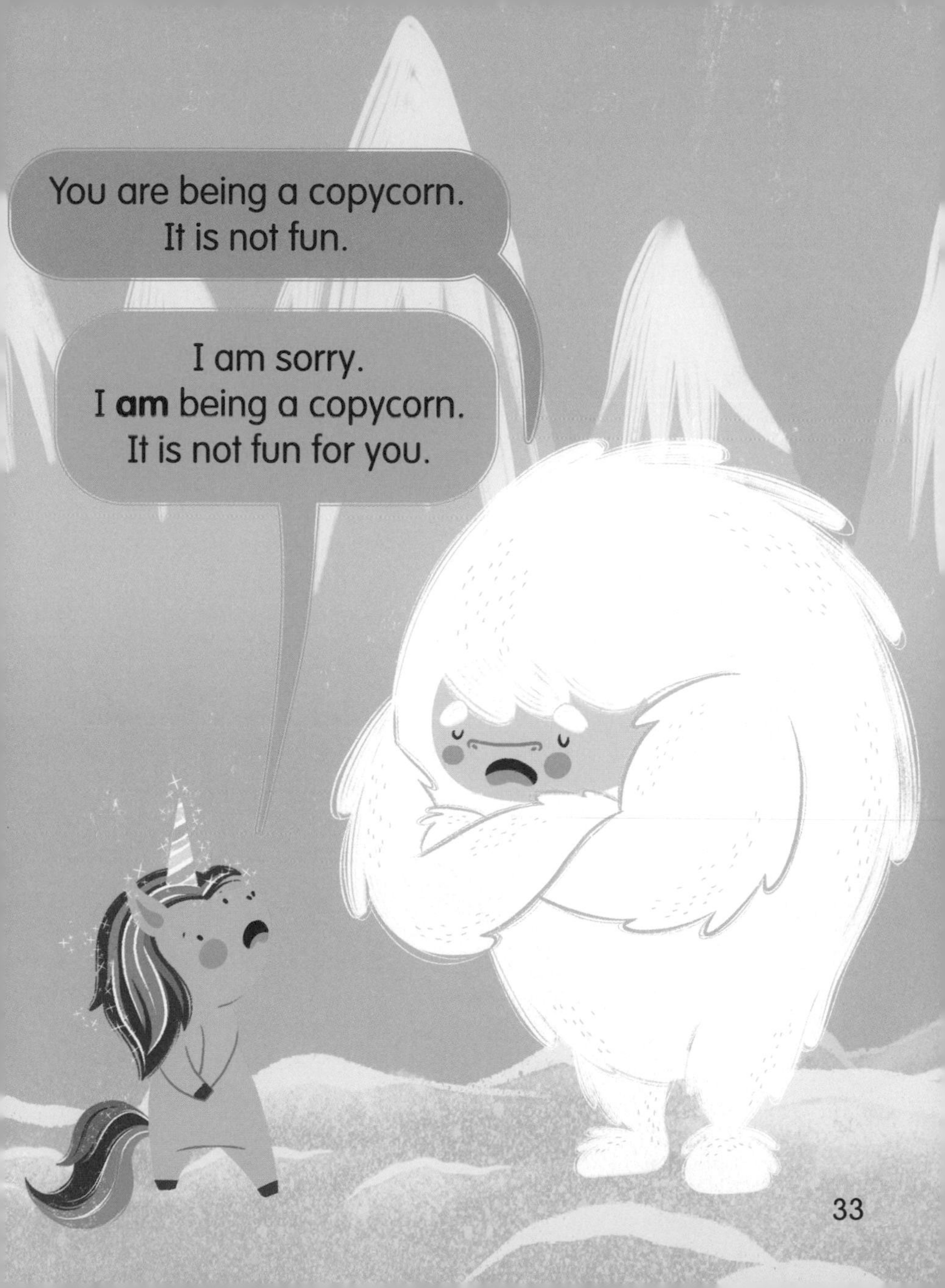
You are being a copycorn. It is not fun.
I am sorry. I **am** being a copycorn. It is not fun for you.

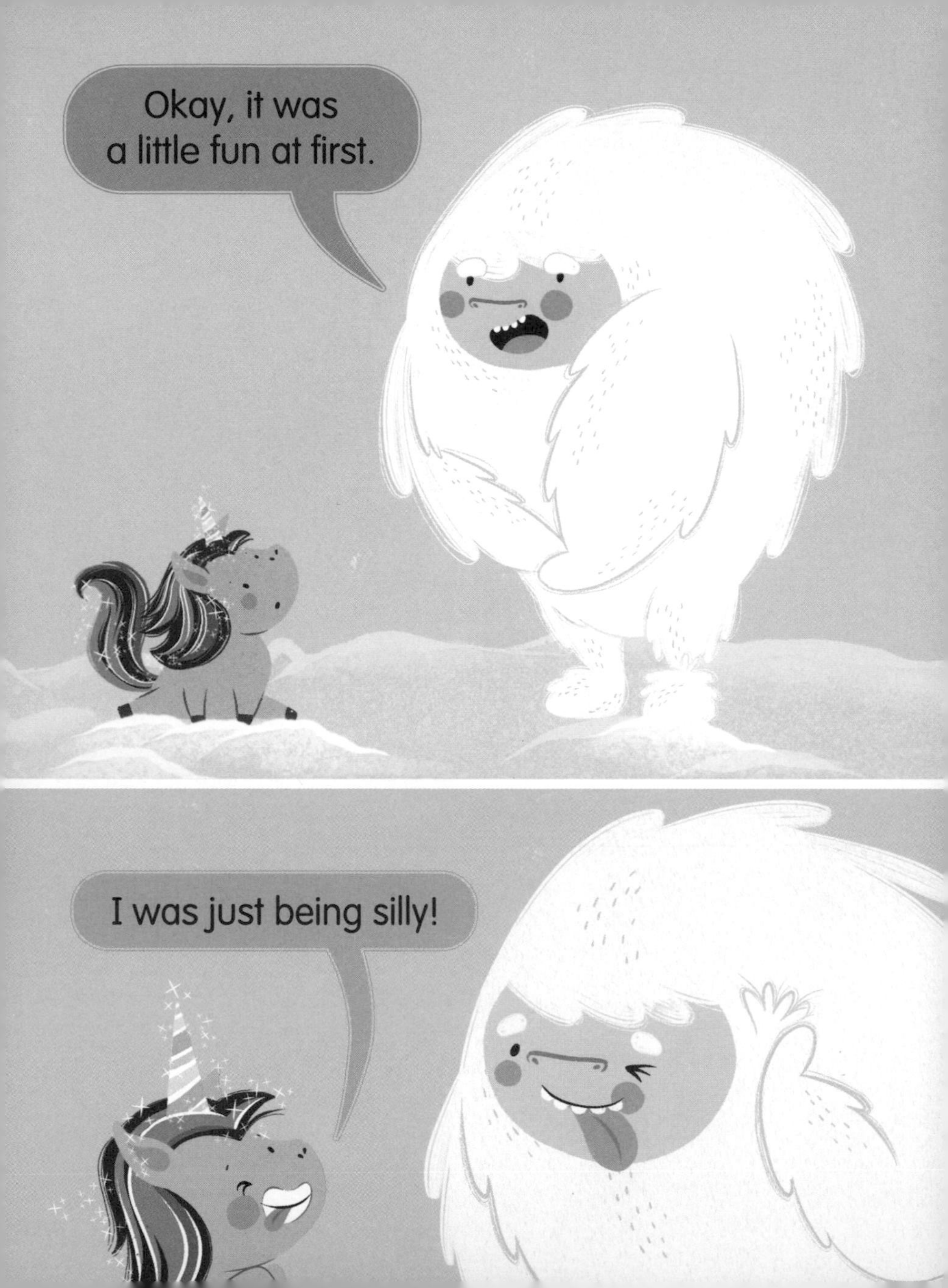
Okay, it was
a little fun at first.
I was just being silly!

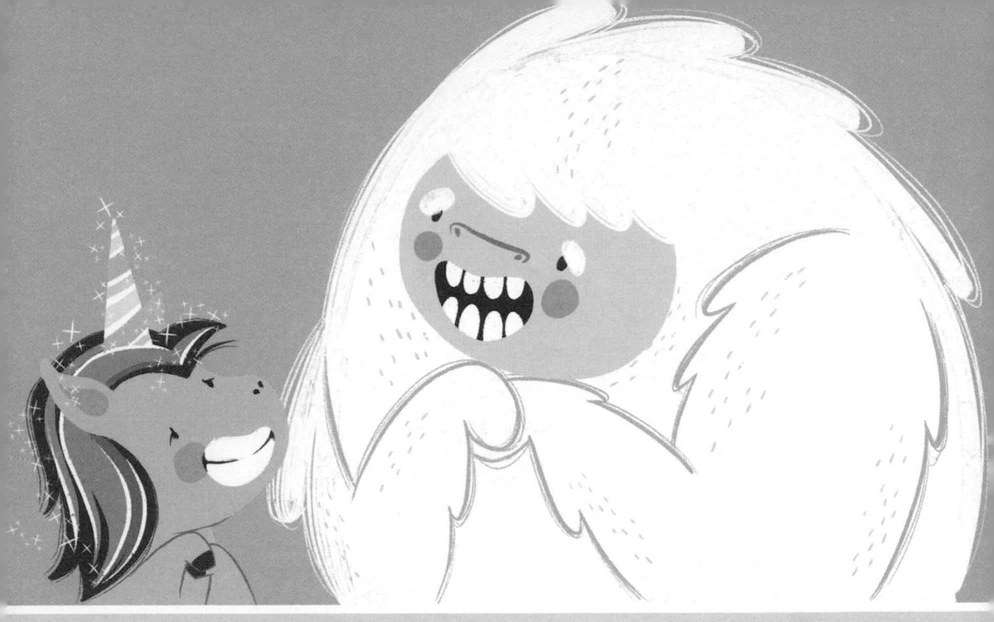

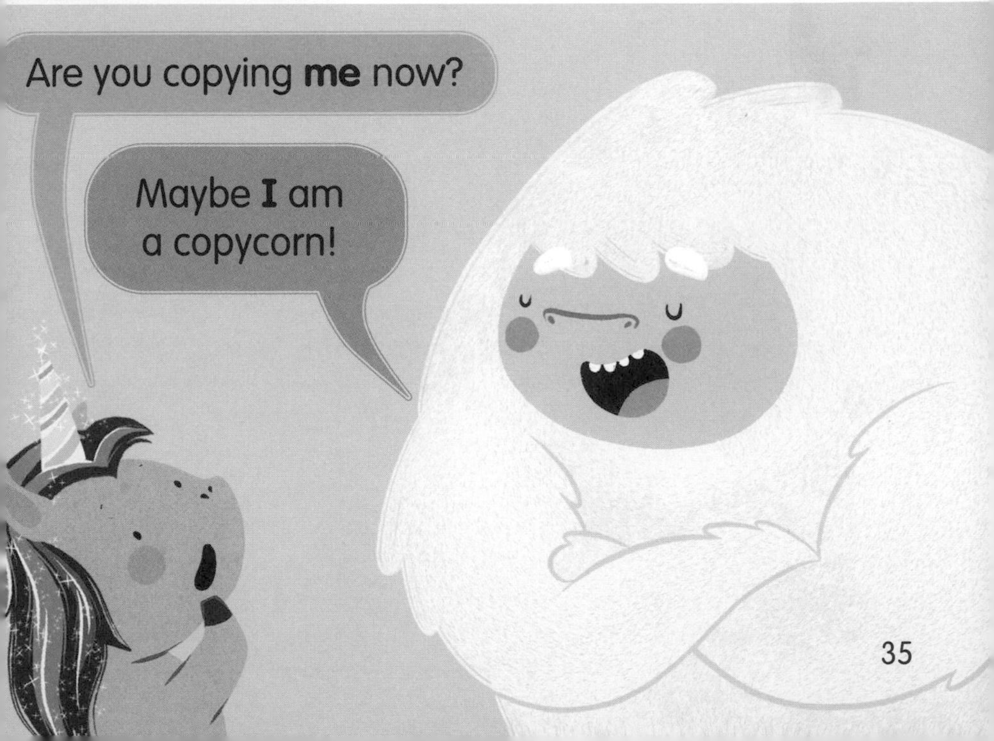
Are you copying **me** now?
Maybe **I** am a copycorn!

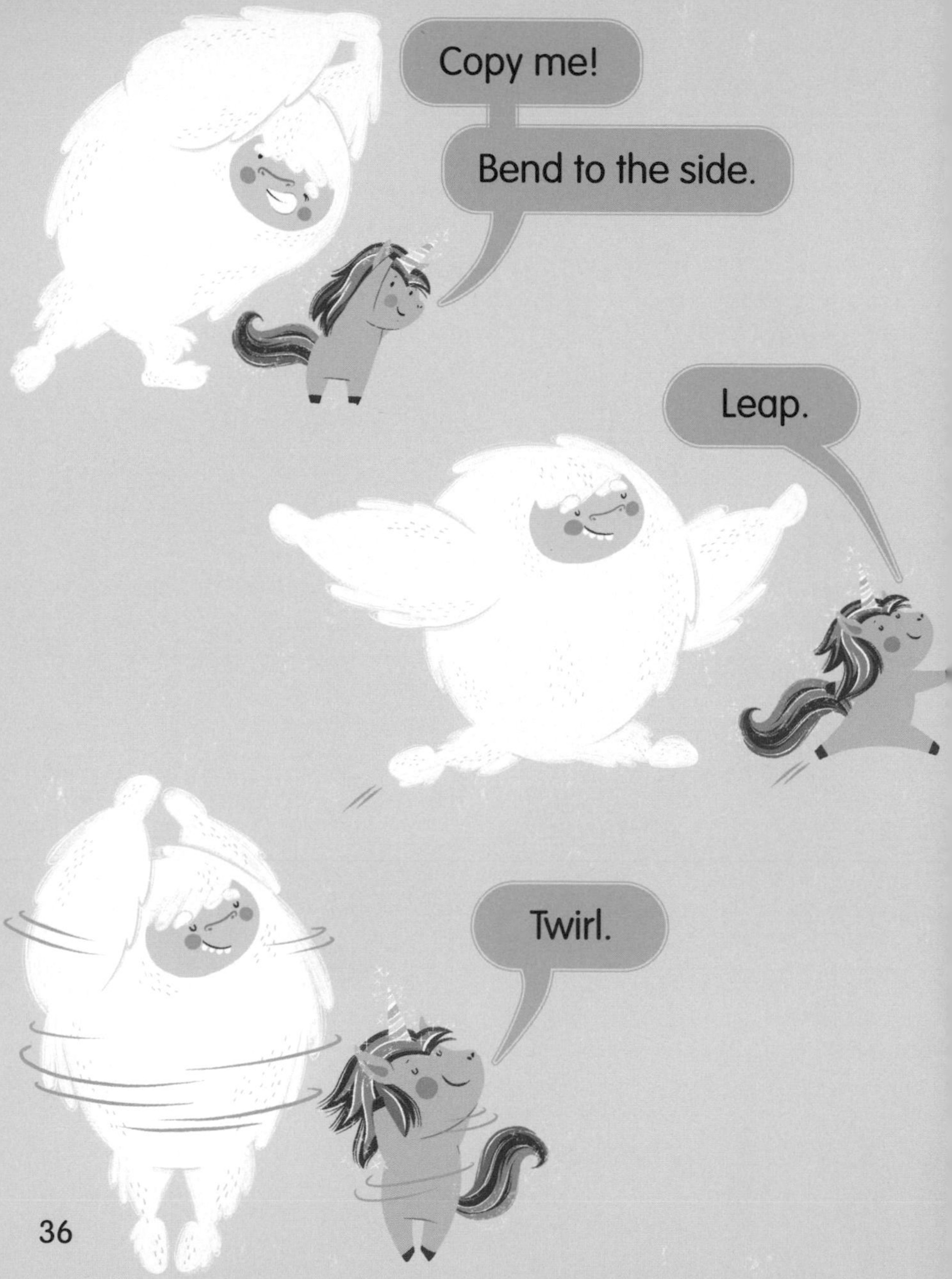
Copy me!
Bend to the side.
Leap.
Twirl.

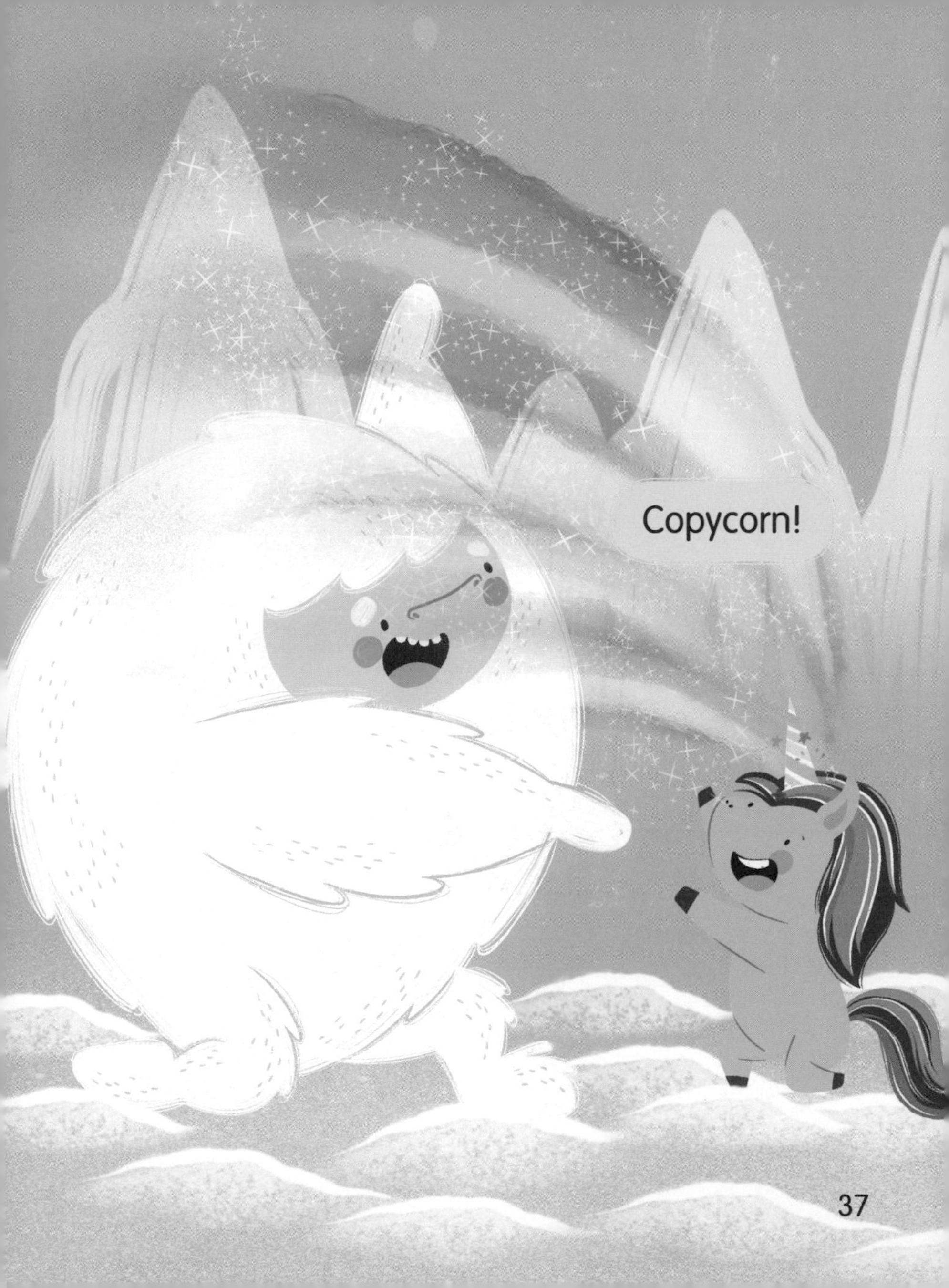
Copycorn!

Tea Party

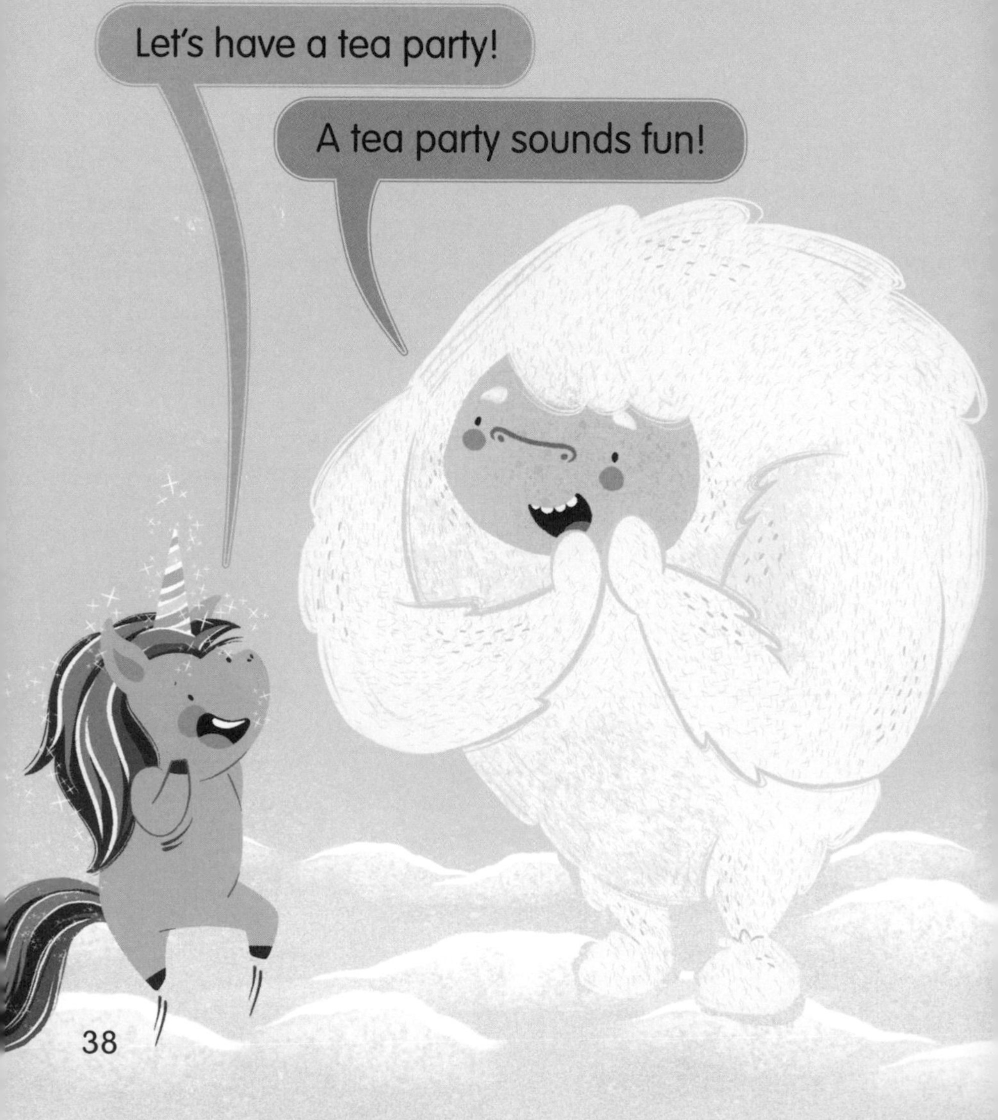
Let's have a tea party!
A tea party sounds fun!

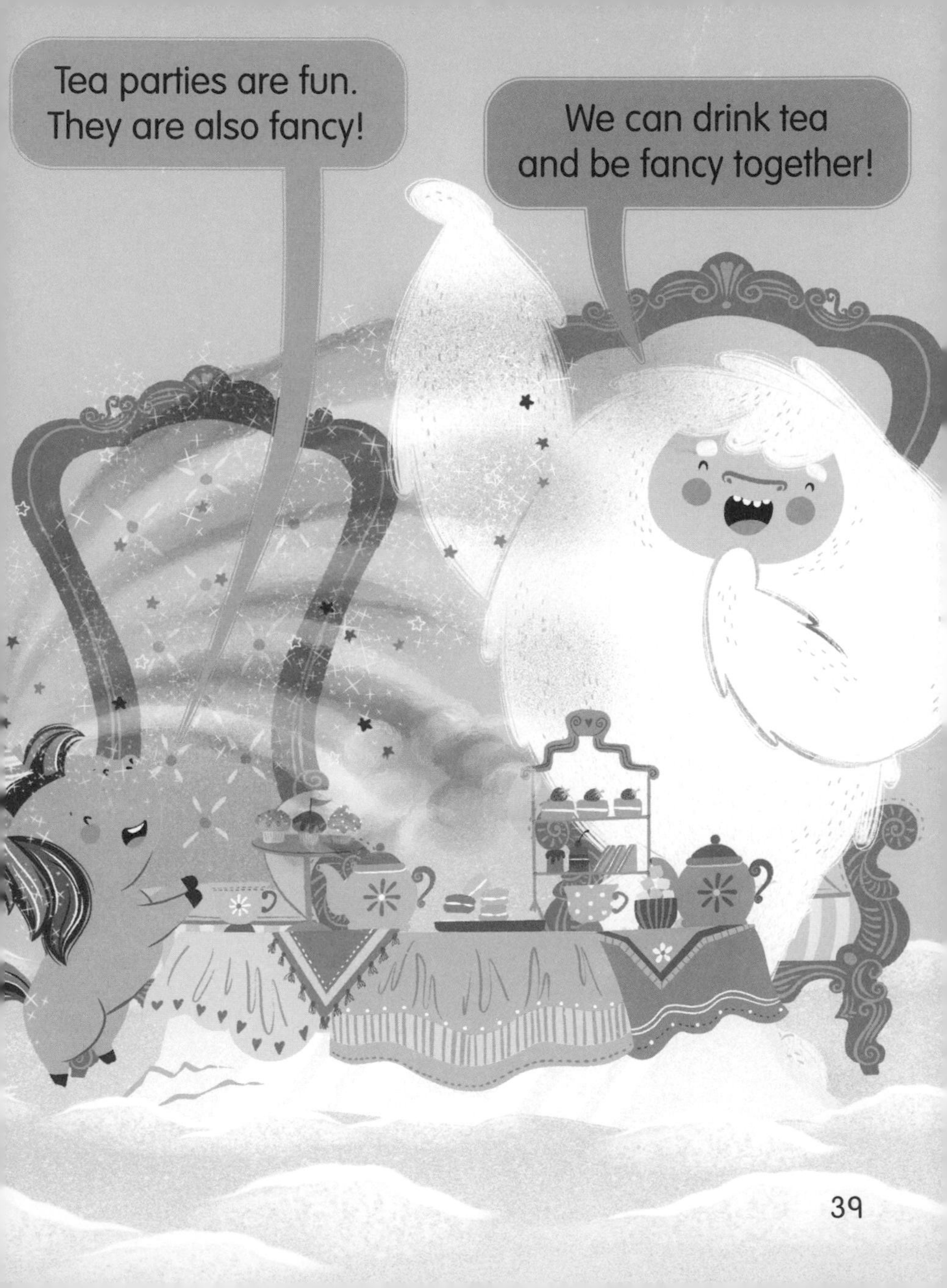
Tea parties are fun.
They are also fancy!
We can drink tea
and be fancy together!

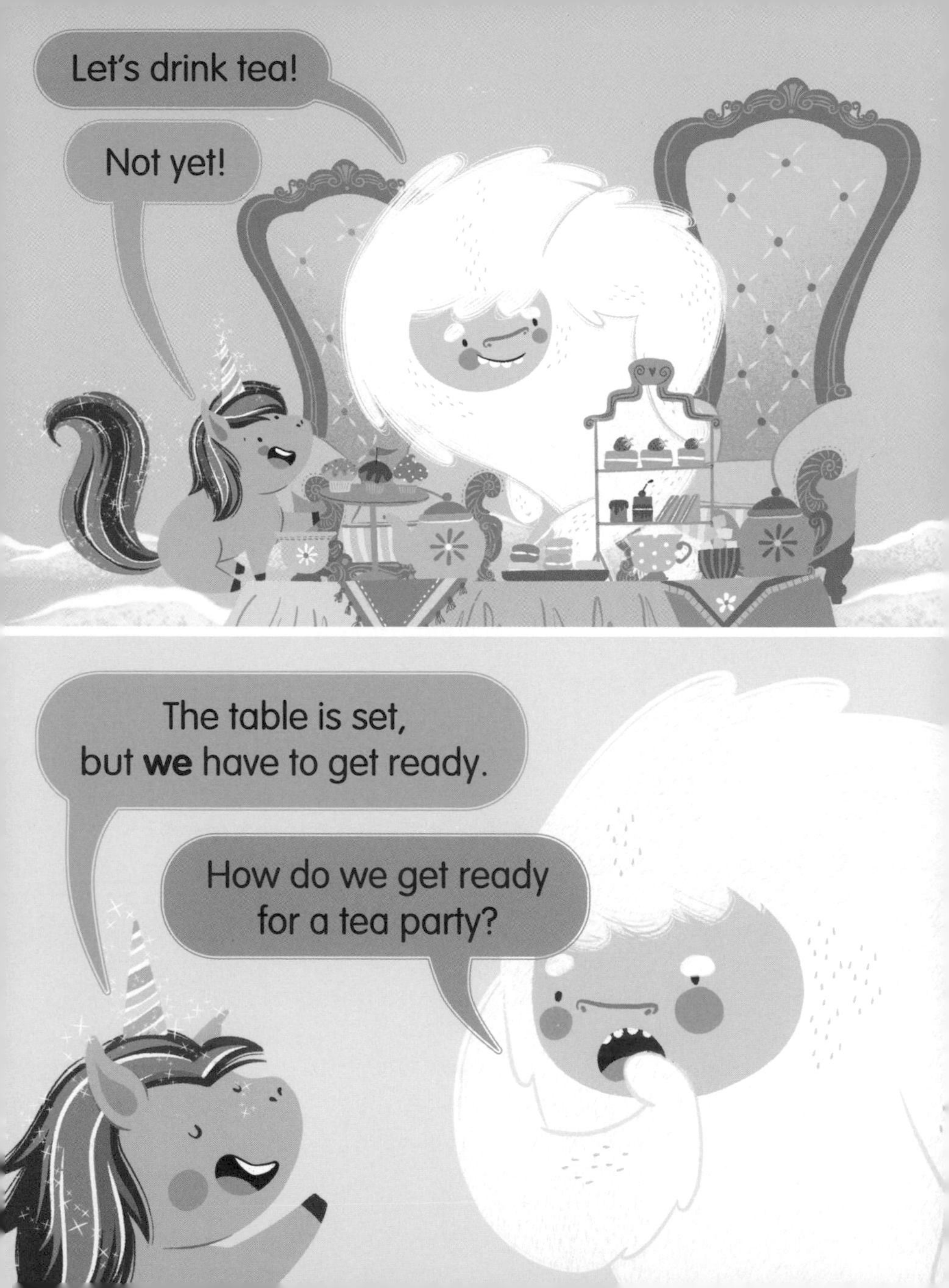
Let's drink tea!
Not yet!
The table is set, but **we** have to get ready.
How do we get ready for a tea party?

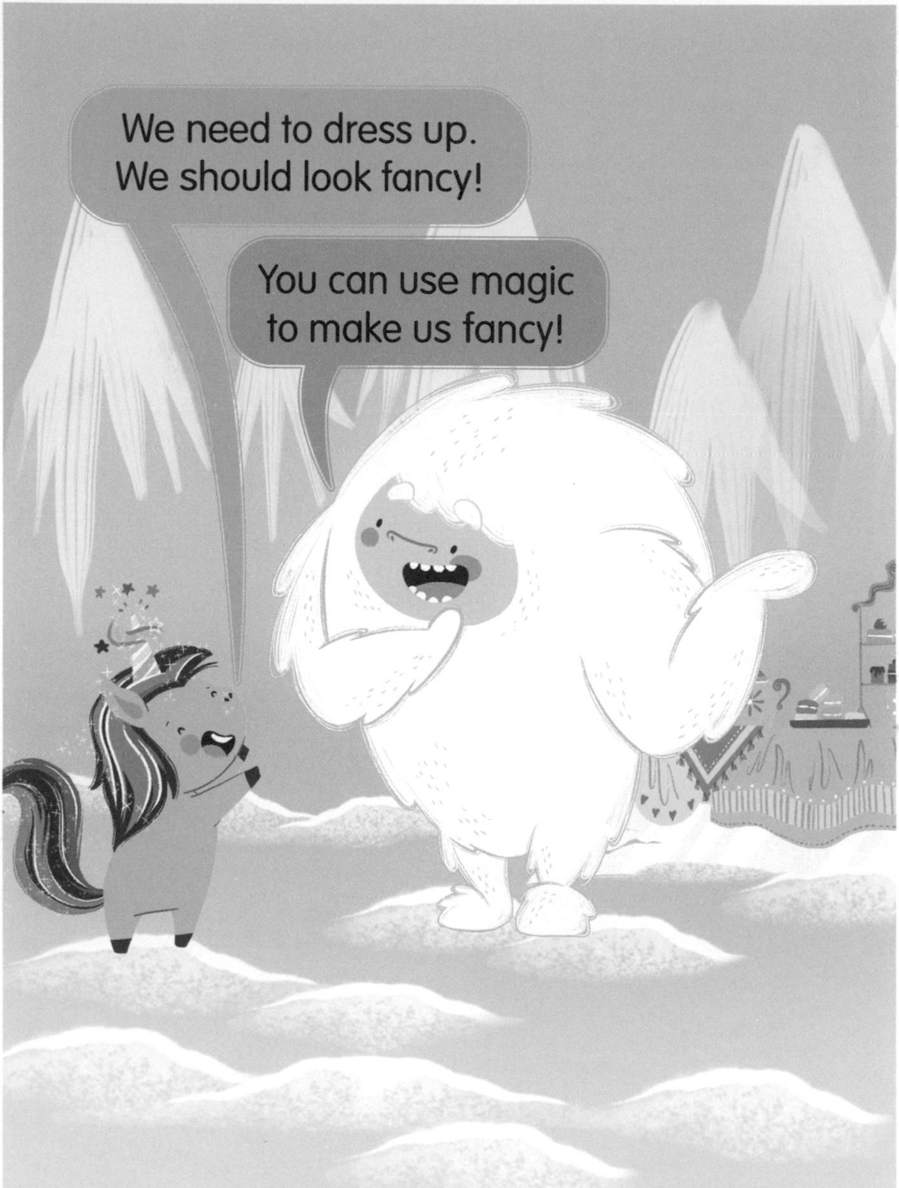
We need to dress up. We should look fancy!
You can use magic to make us fancy!

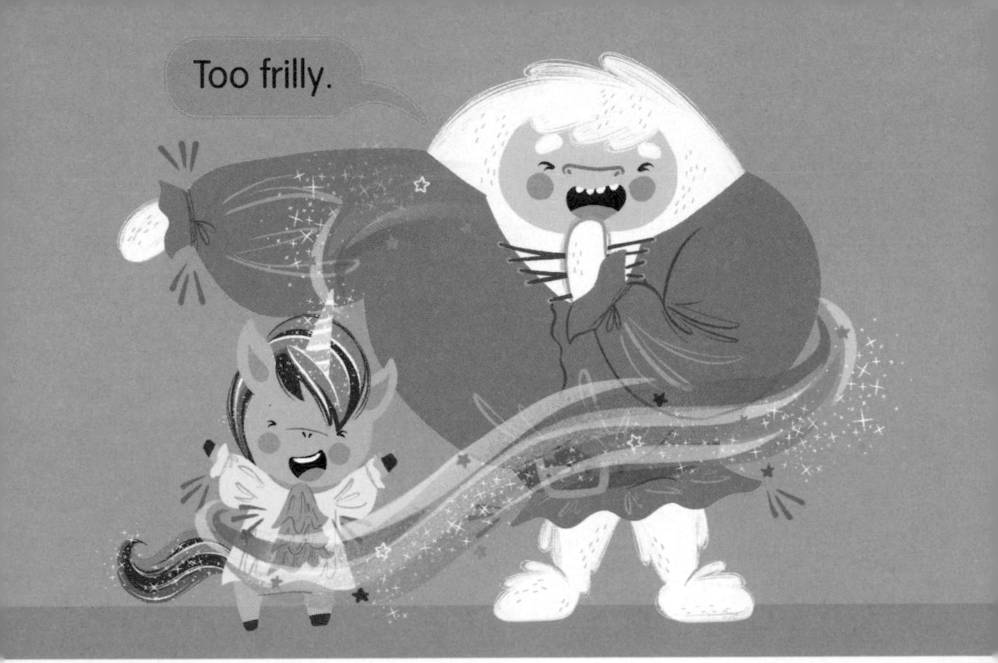
Too frilly.

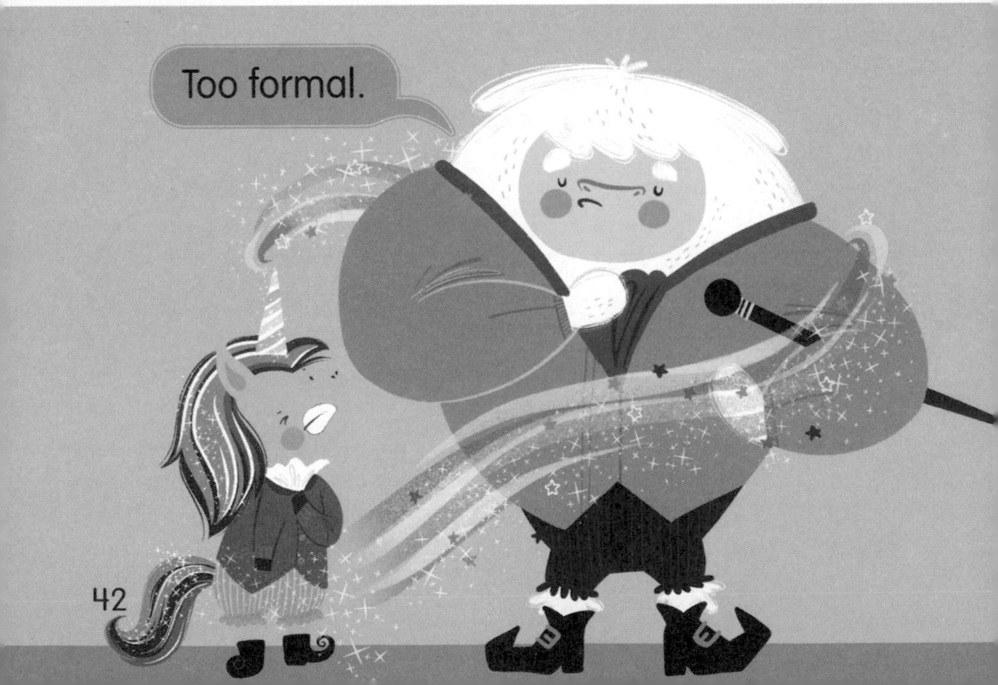
Too formal.

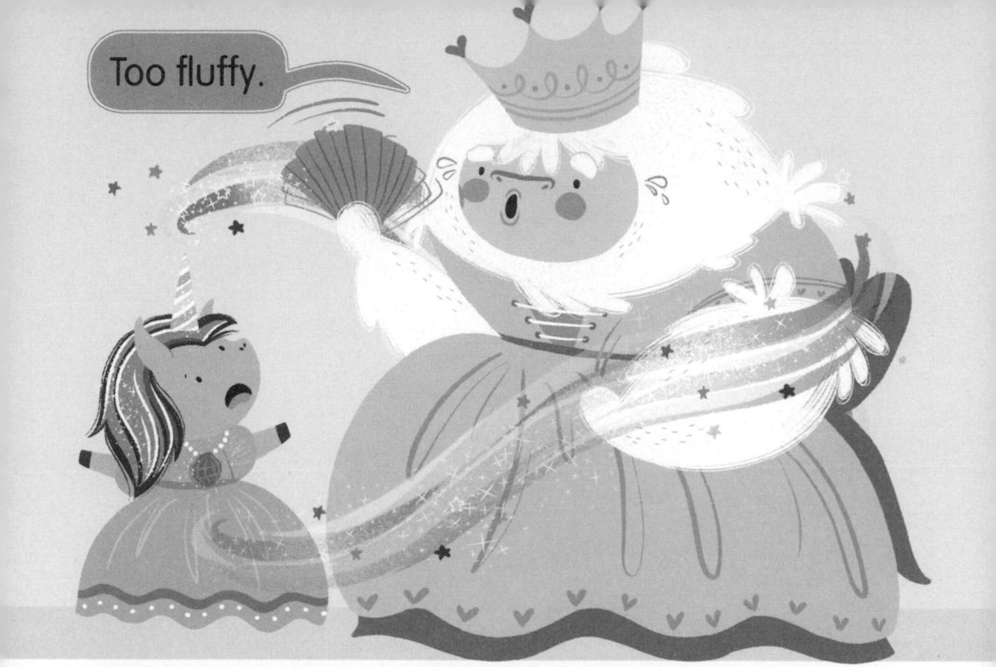
Too fluffy.

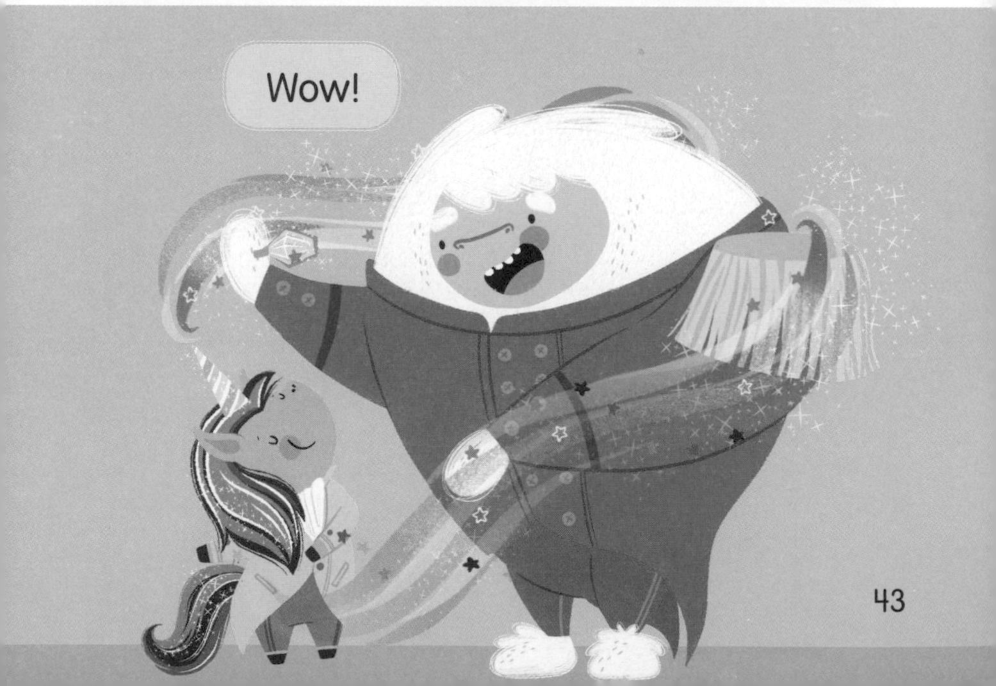
Wow!

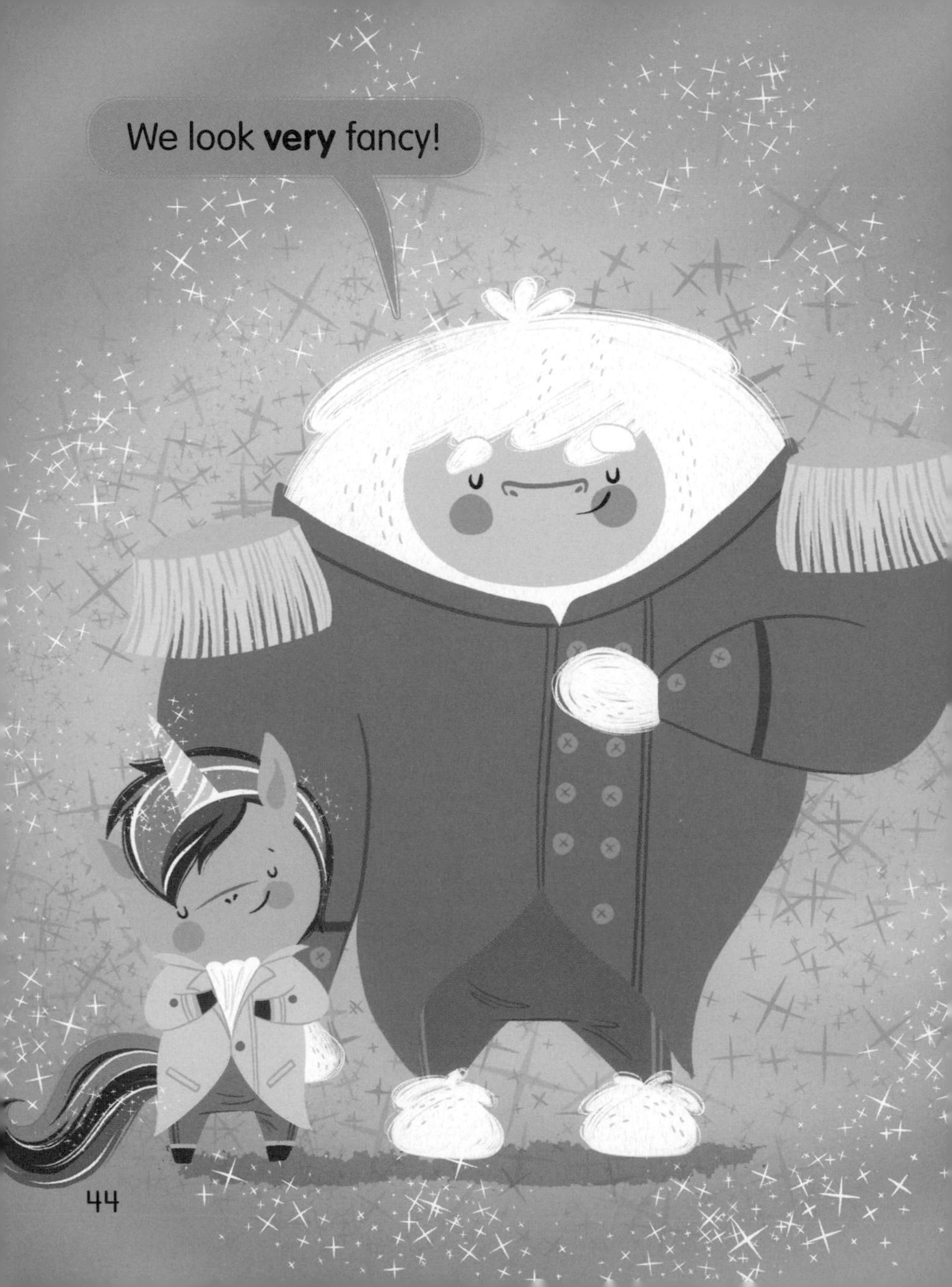
We look **very** fancy!

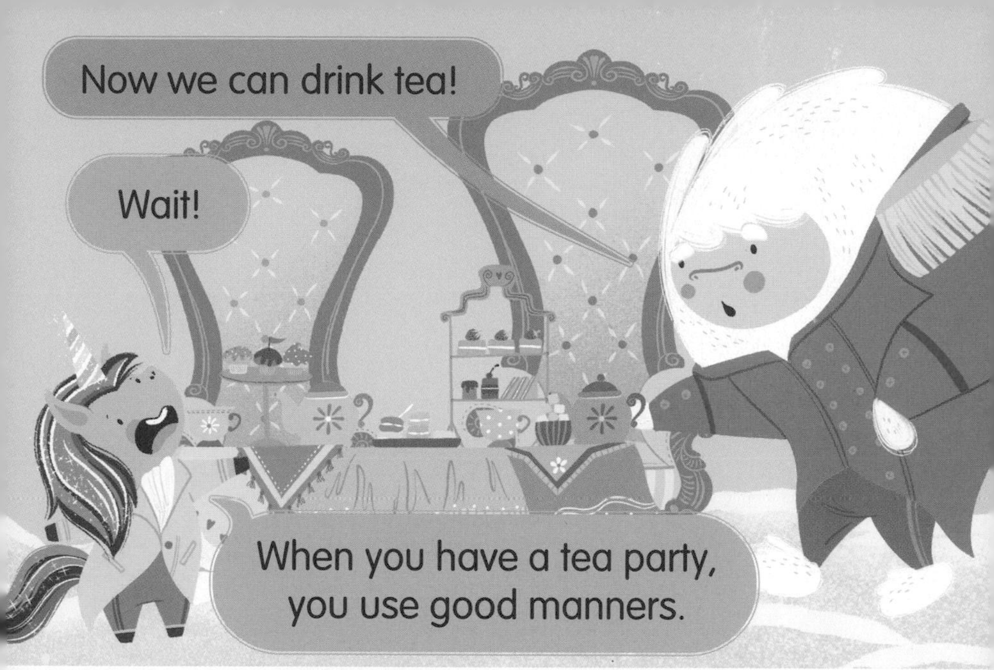
Now we can drink tea!
Wait!
When you have a tea party,
you use good manners.

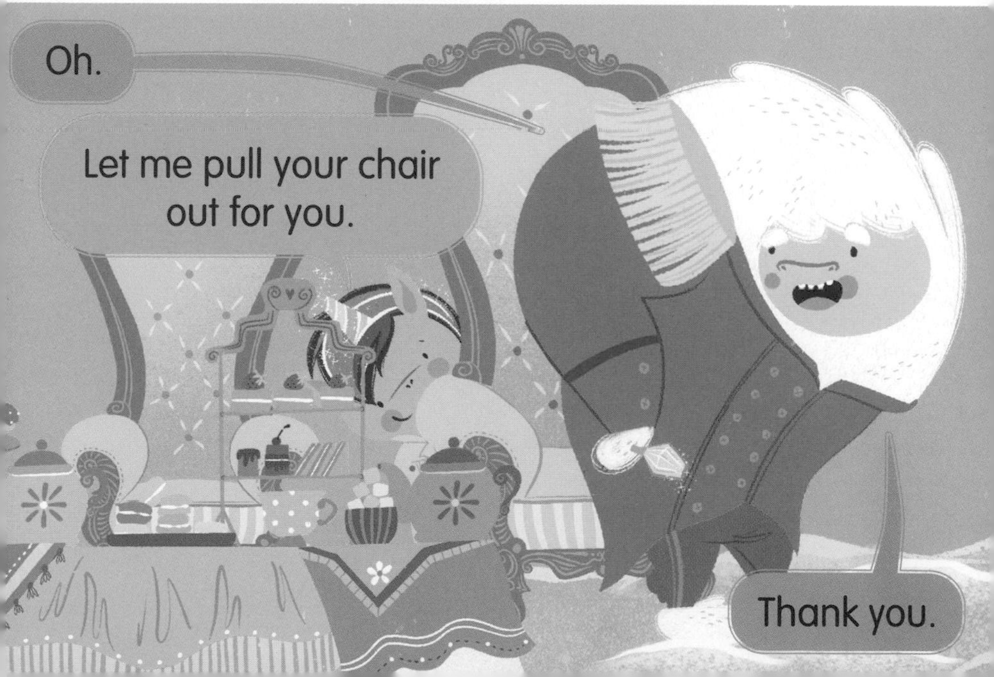
Oh.
Let me pull your chair
out for you.
Thank you.

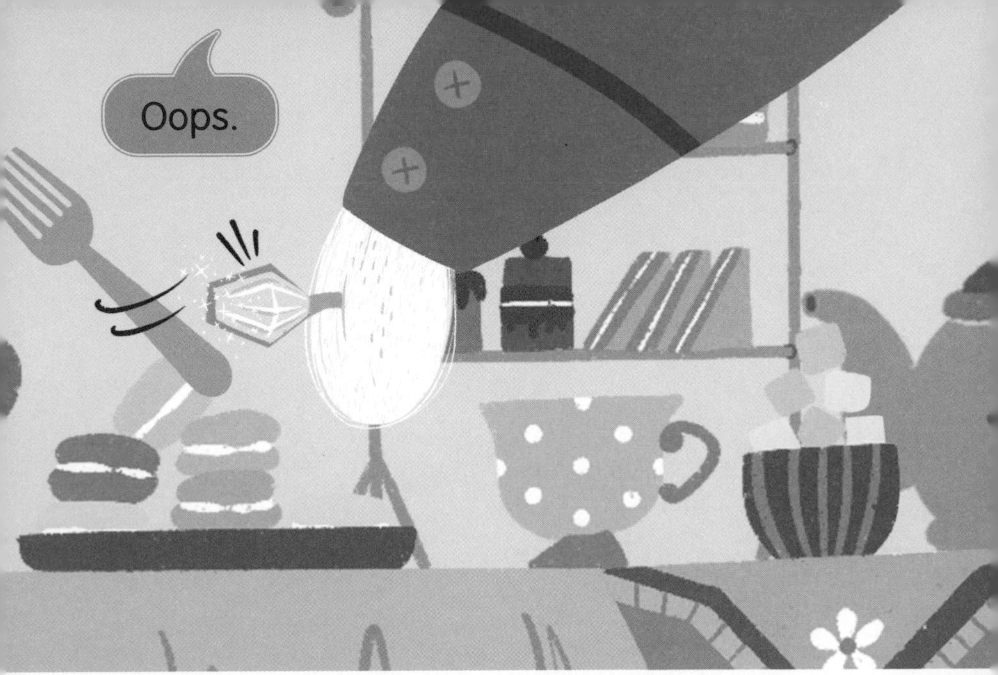
Oops.

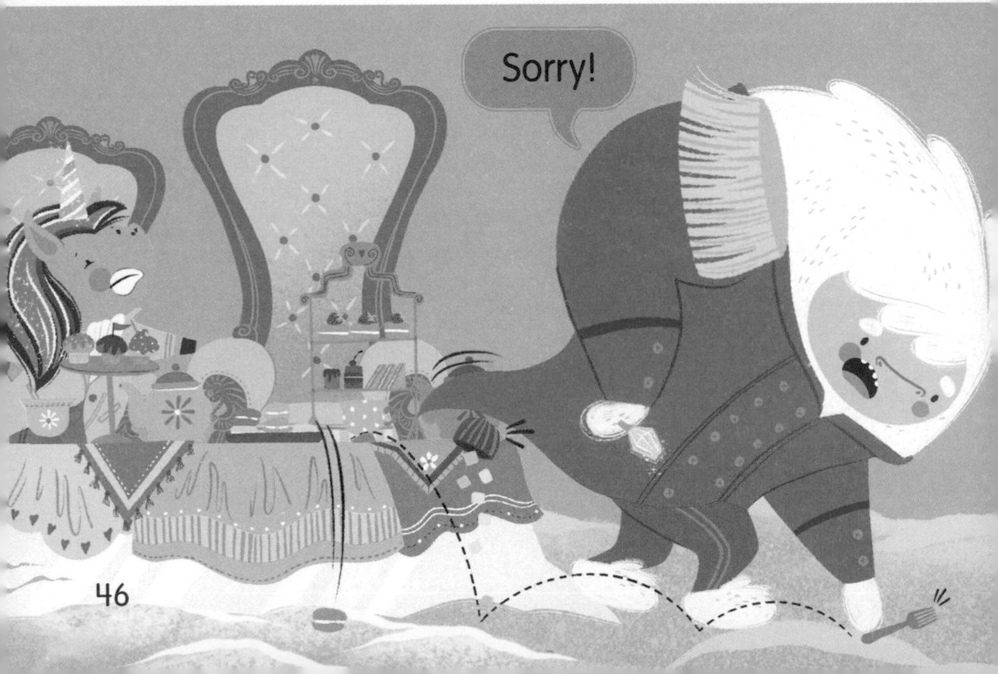
Sorry!

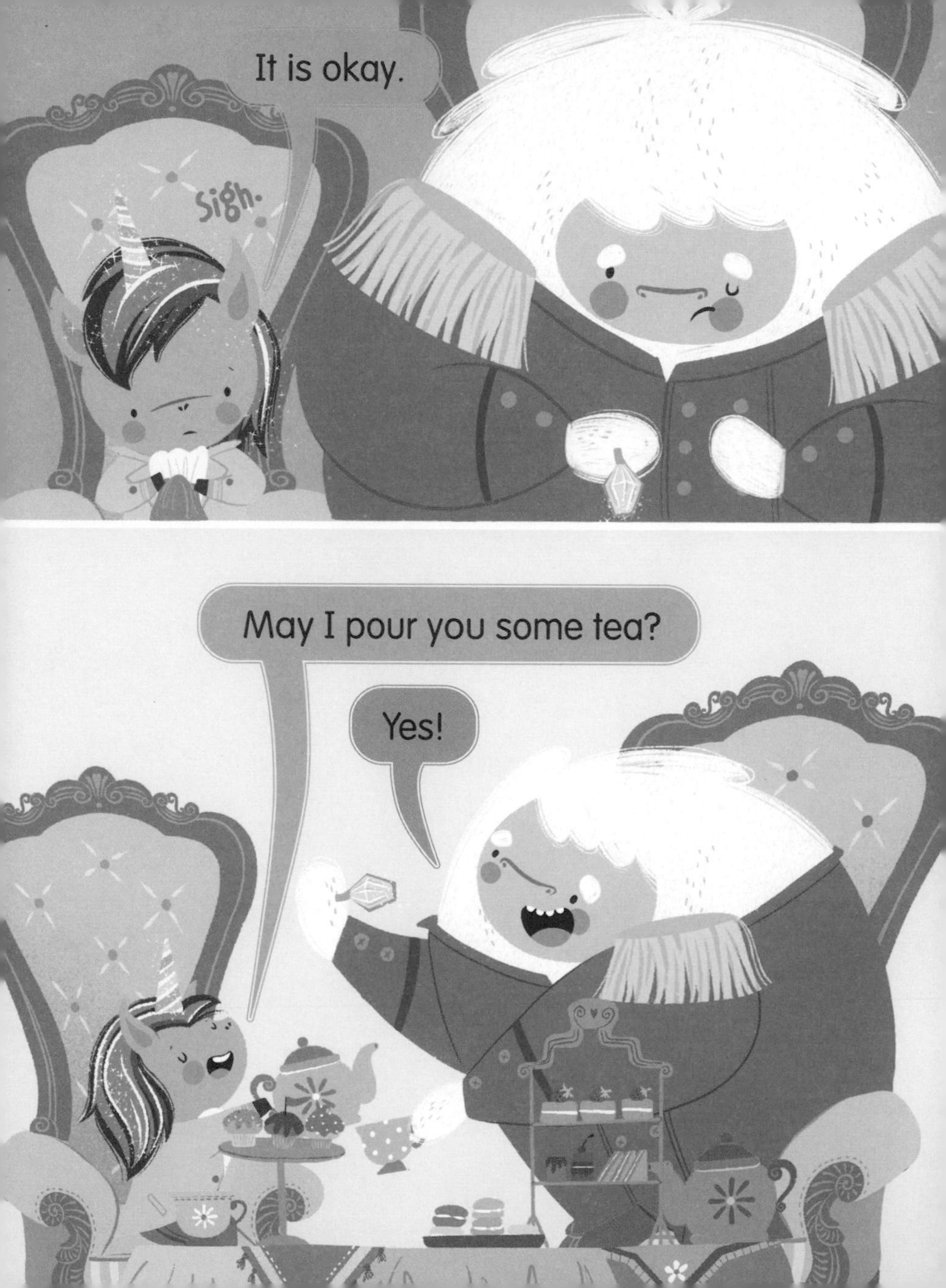
It is okay.
Sigh.
May I pour you some tea?
Yes!

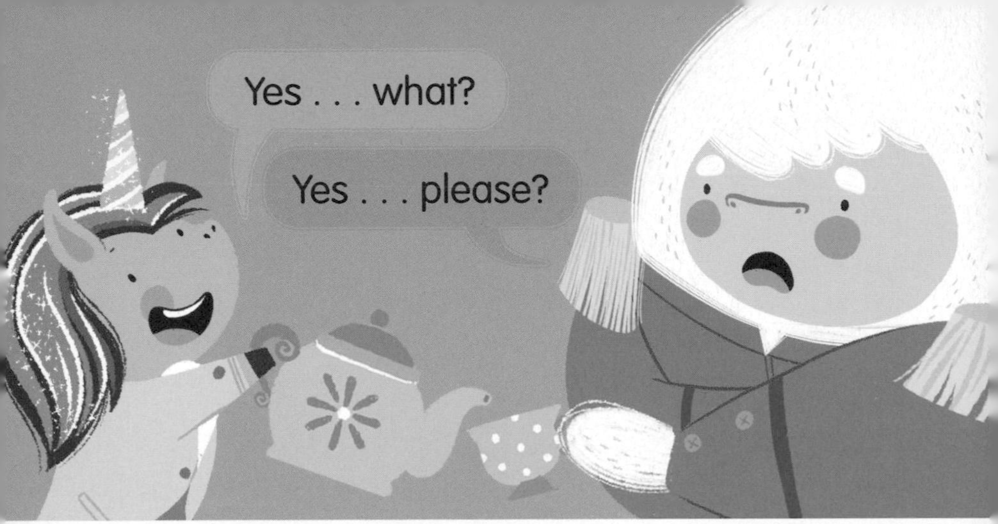
Yes . . . what?
Yes . . . please?
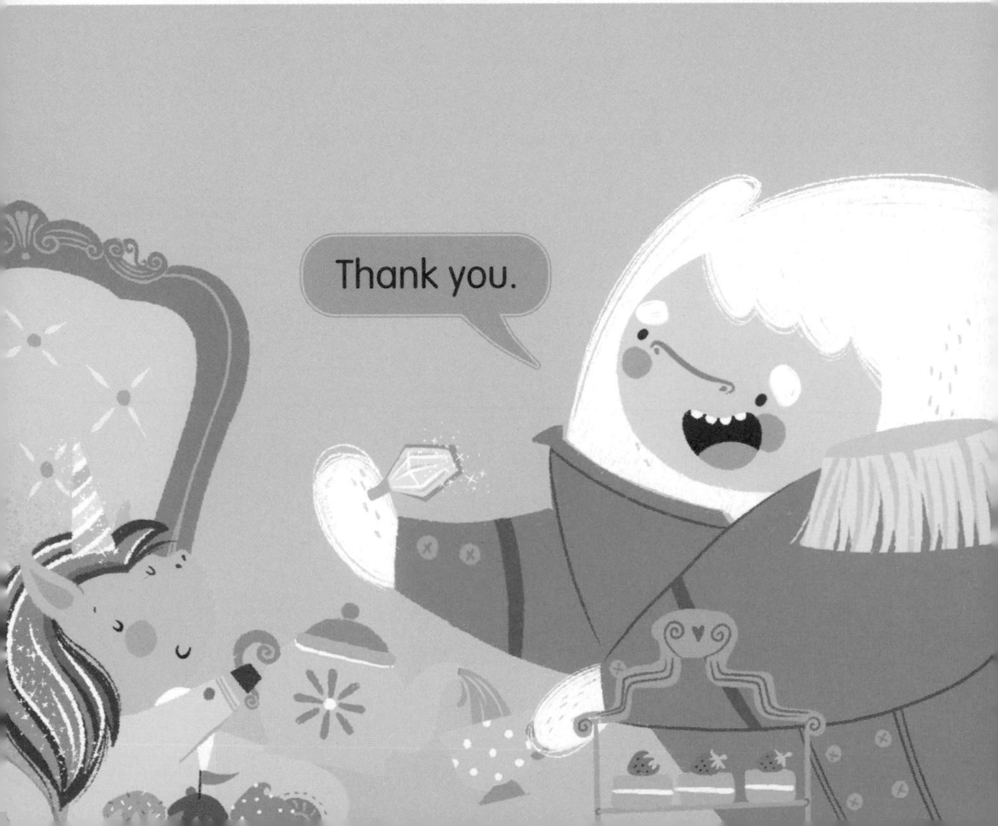
Thank you.

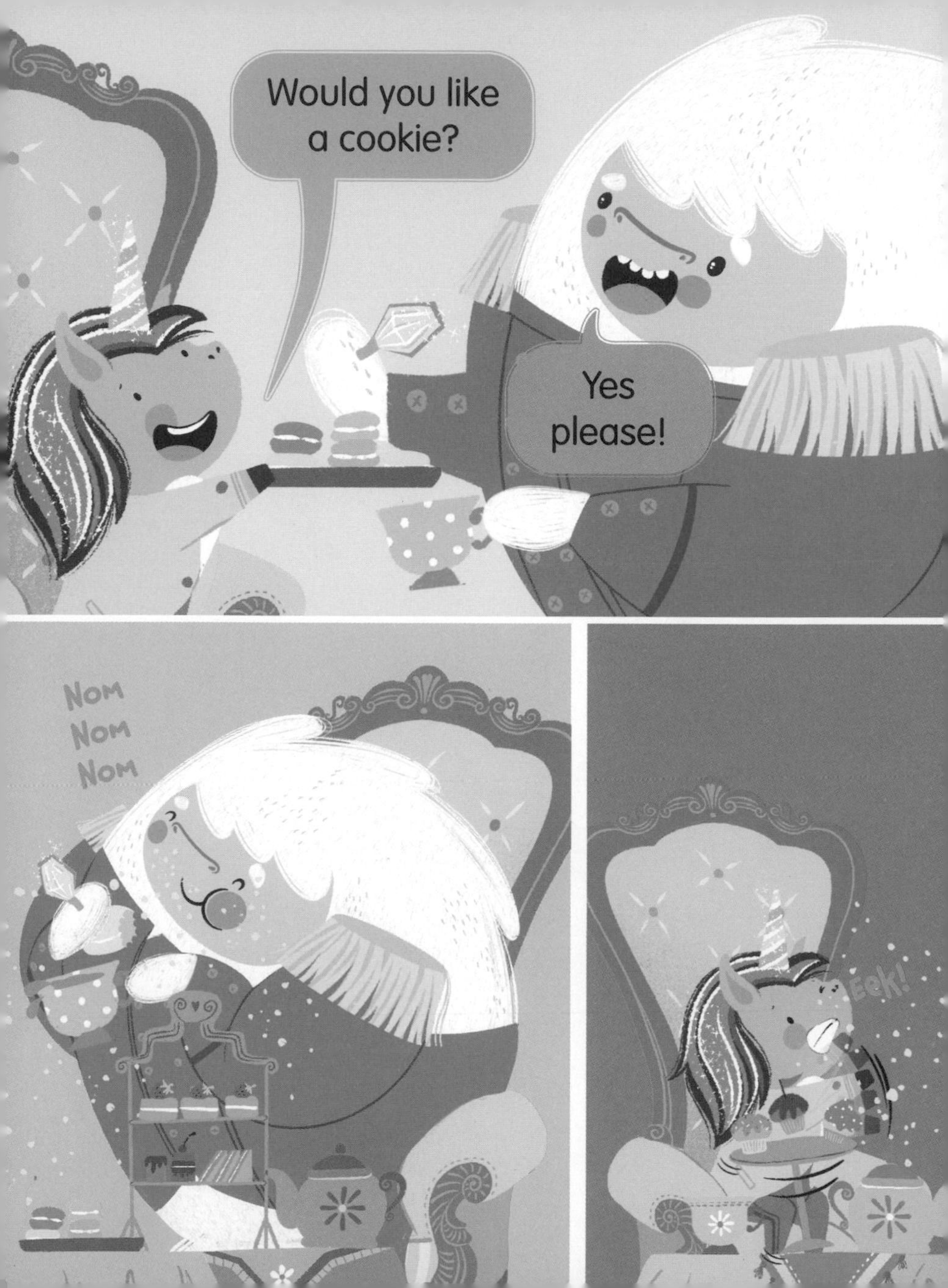
Would you like a cookie?
Yes please!
Nom
Nom
Nom
Eek!

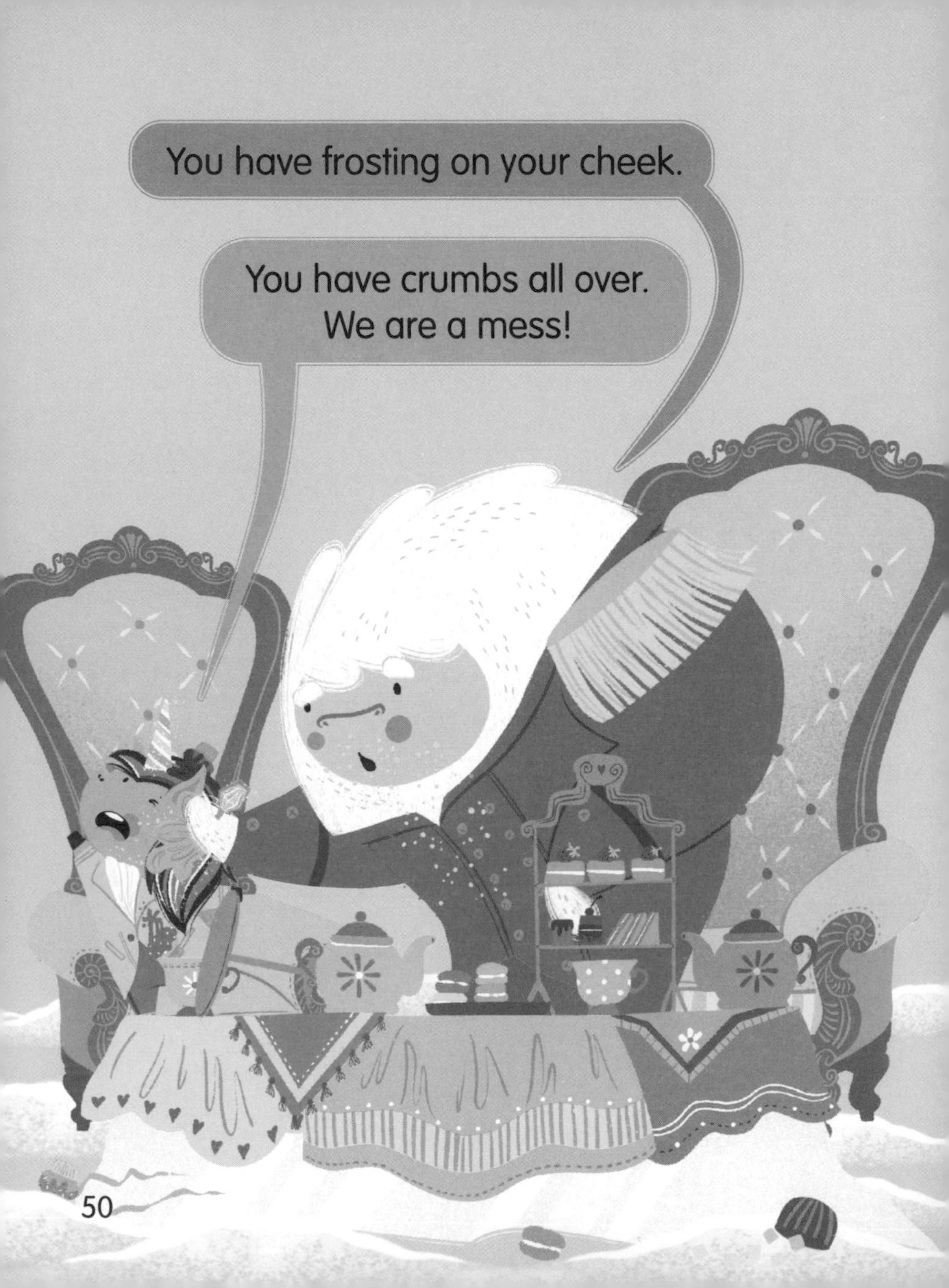
You have frosting on your cheek.
You have crumbs all over. We are a mess!

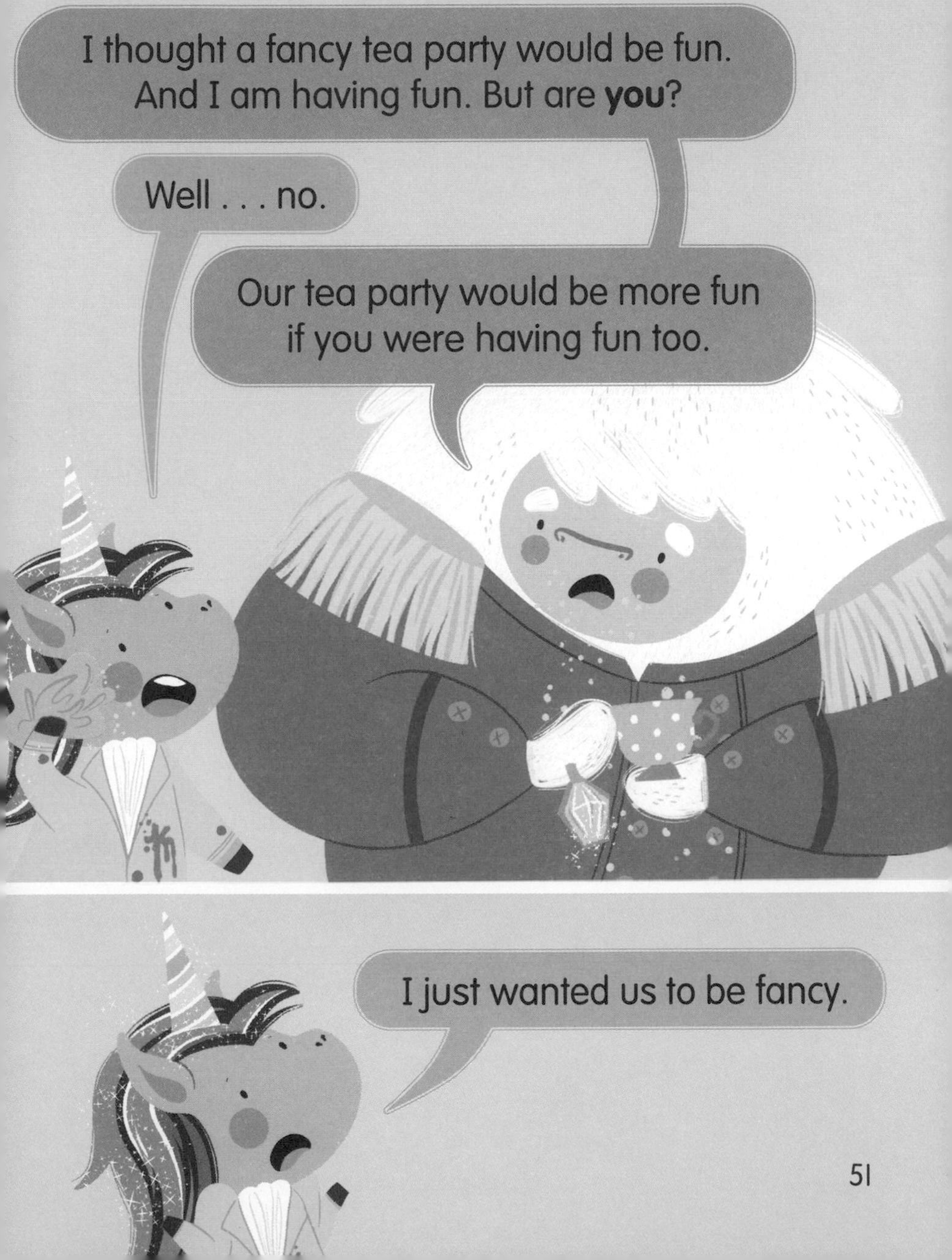
I thought a fancy tea party would be fun. And I am having fun. But are **you**?
Well . . . no.
Our tea party would be more fun if you were having fun too.
I just wanted us to be fancy.

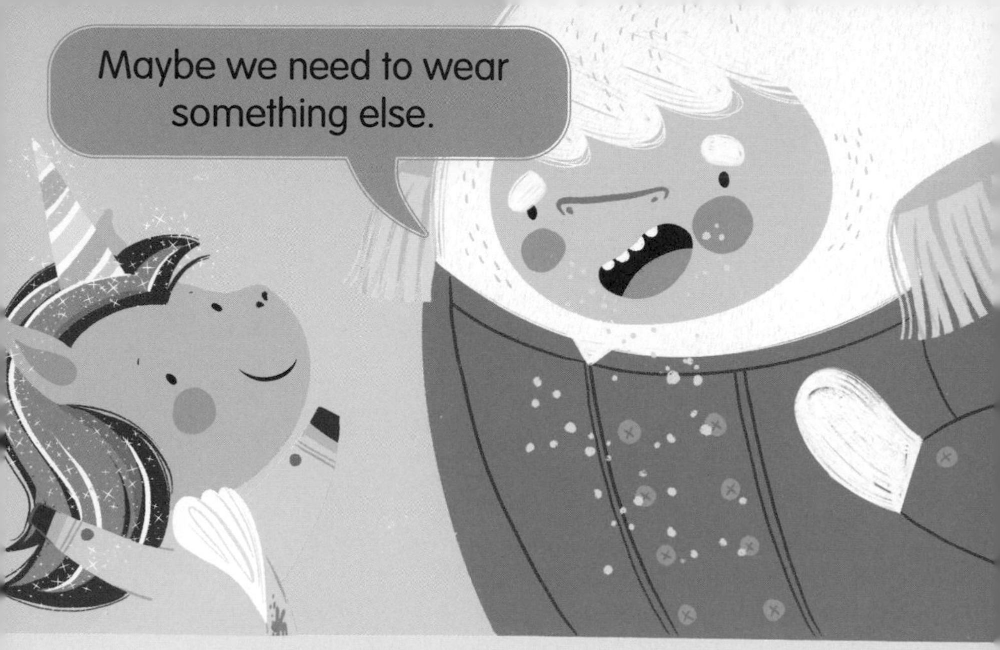
Maybe we need to wear
something else.

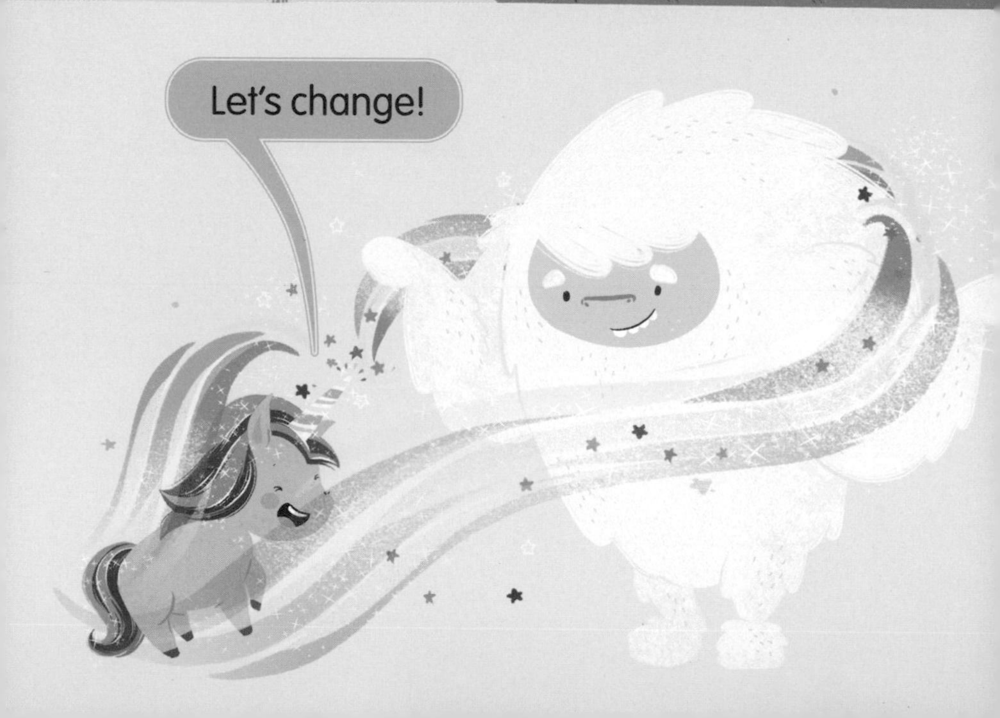
Let's change!

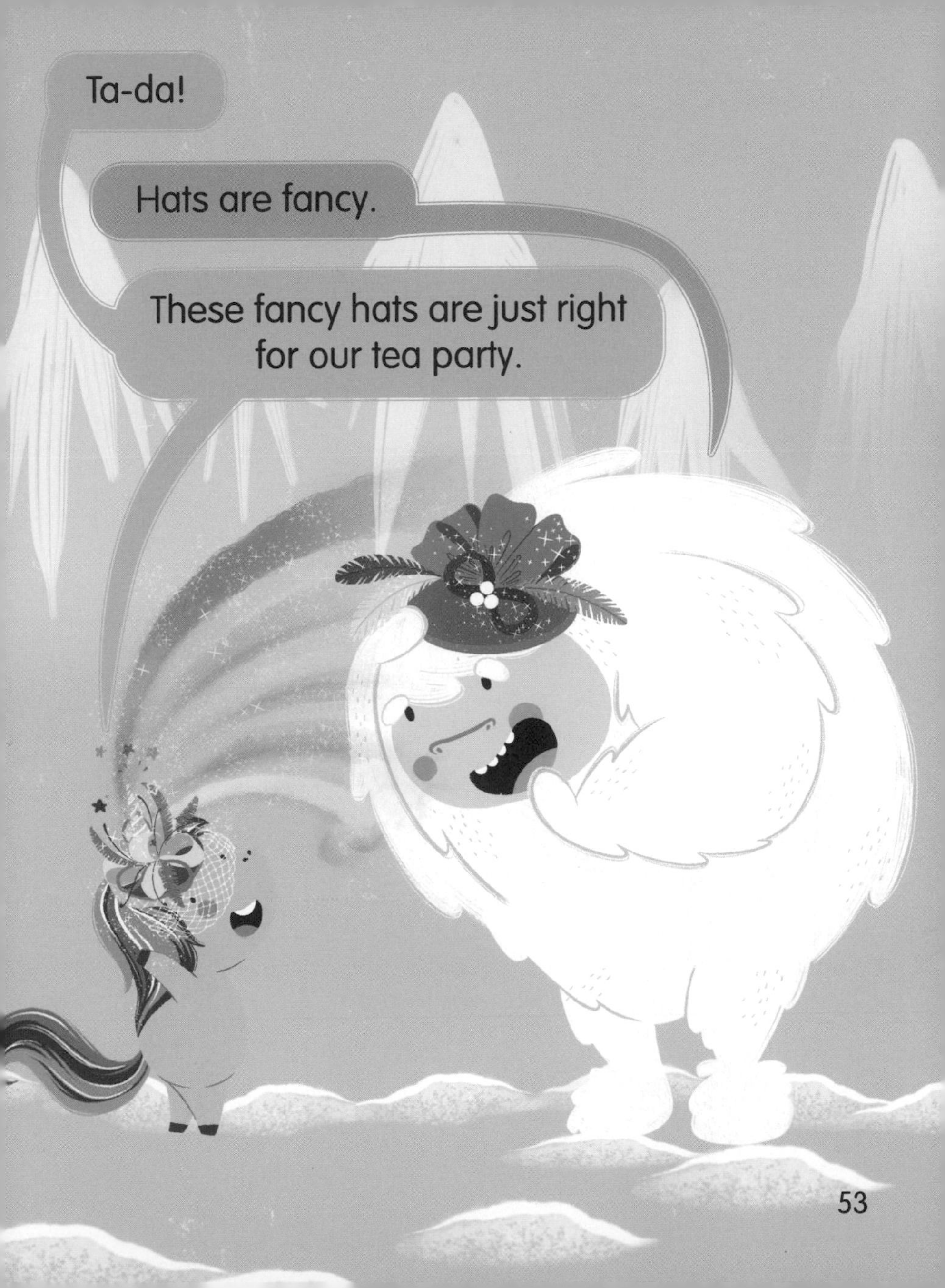
Ta-da!
Hats are fancy.
These fancy hats are just right for our tea party.

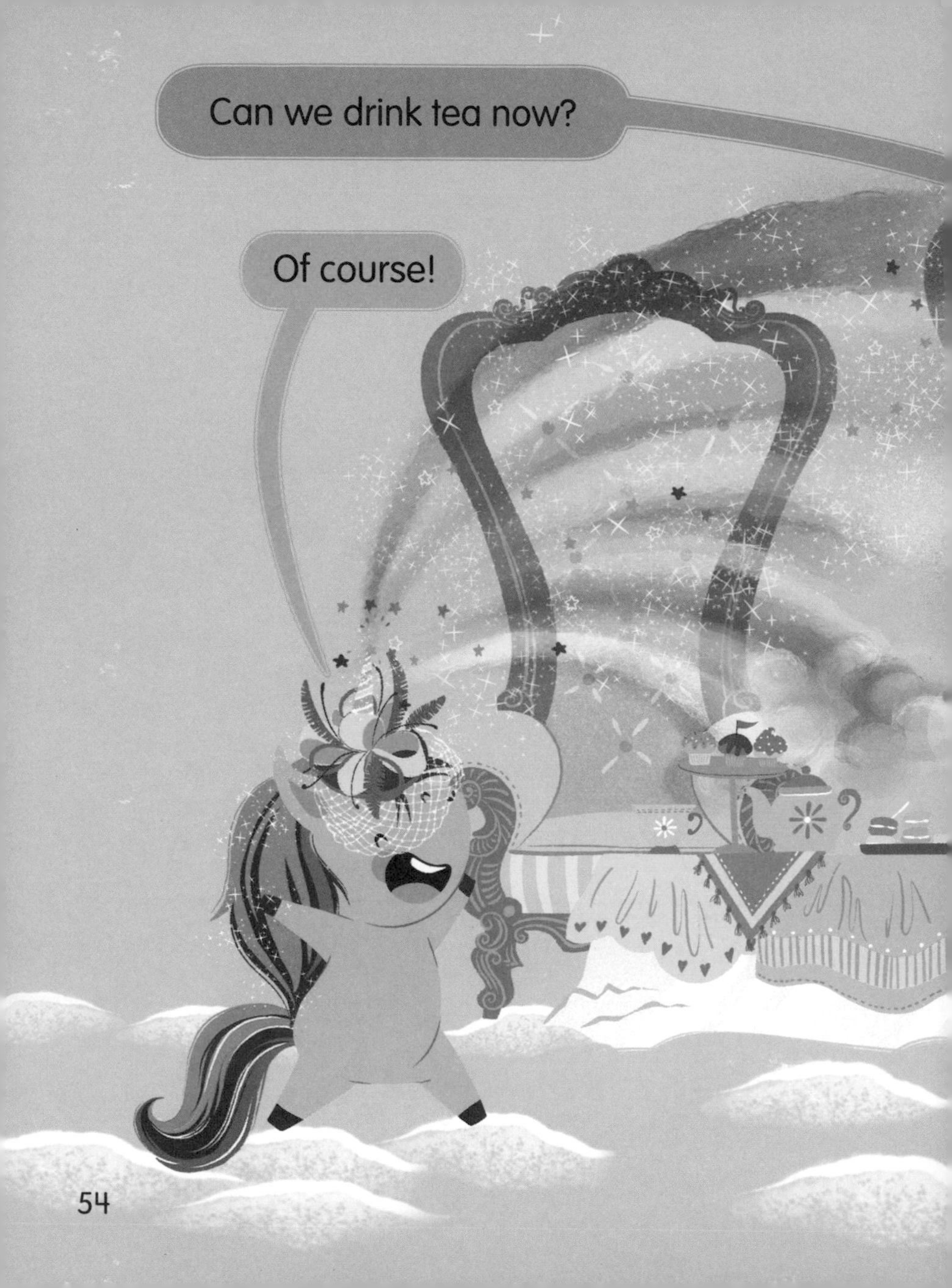
Can we drink tea now?
Of course!

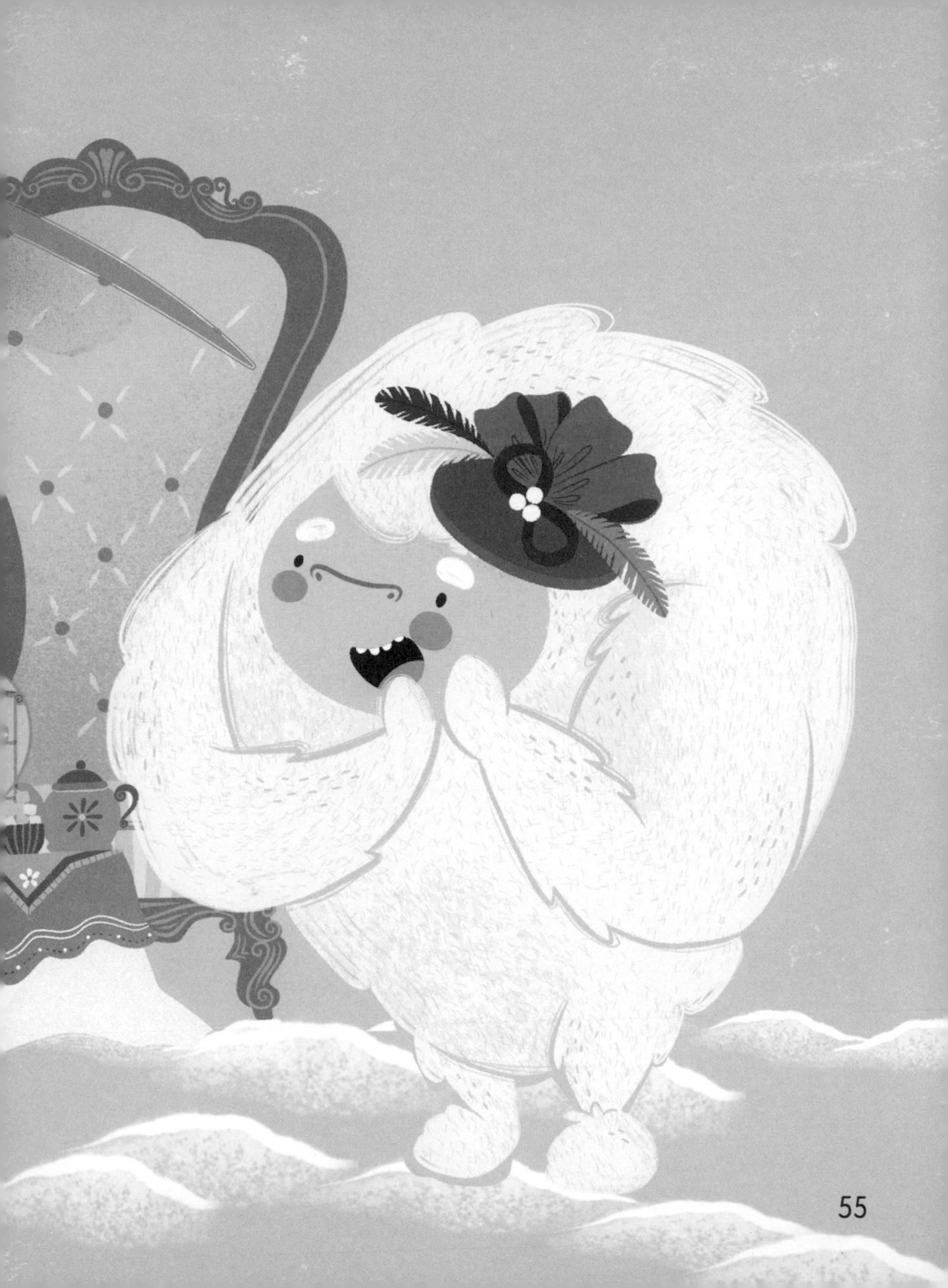

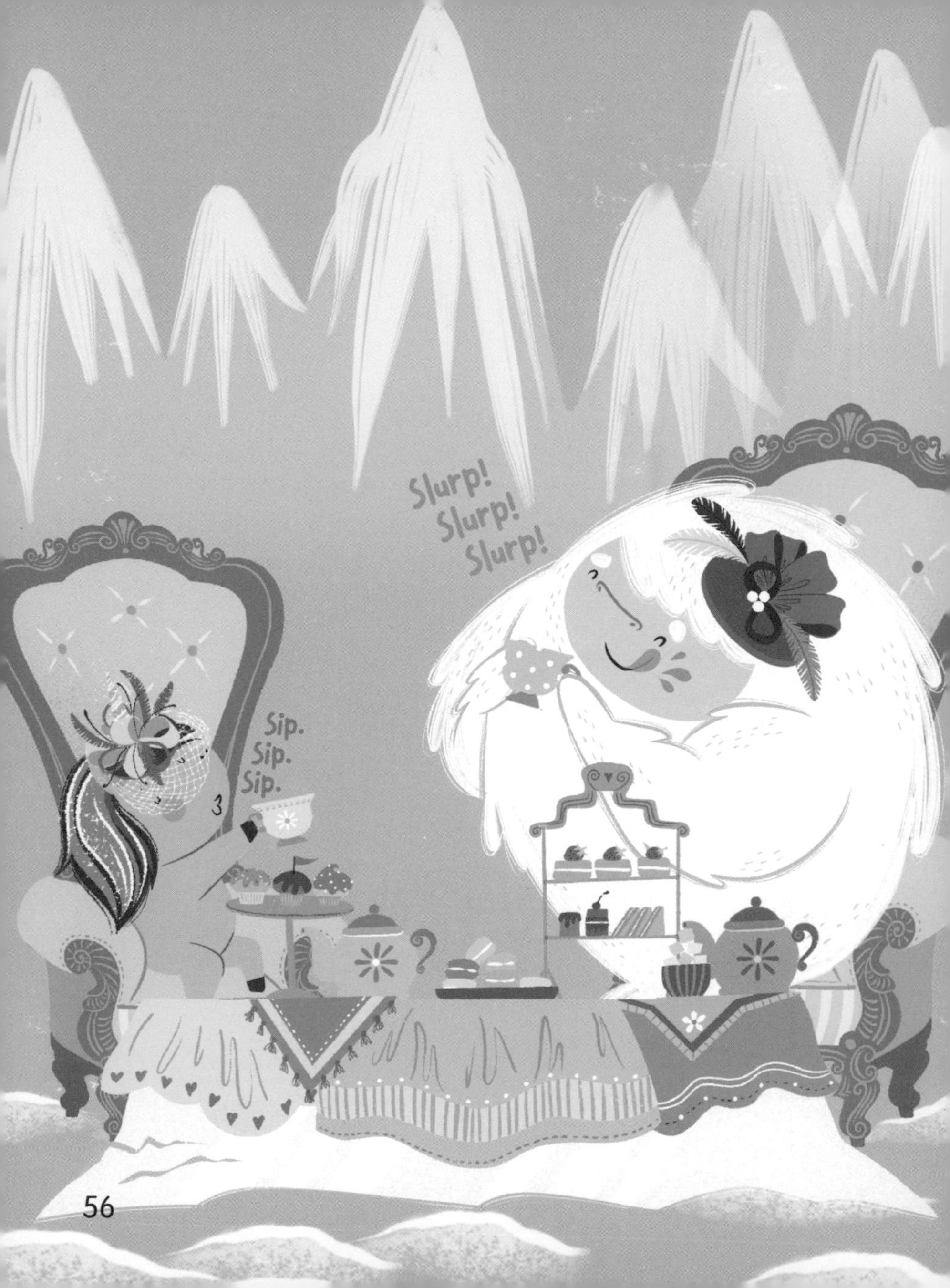
Slurp!
Slurp!
Slurp!
Sip.
Sip.
Sip.

About the Creators

Heather Ayris Burnell loves drinking tea, especially if it means she gets to dress up and have a tea party with a friend! Heather lives on a farm in Washington State where she likes to watch clouds, seeds, and bugs zip, zigzag, and

zoom around in the sky. Heather is a librarian and the author of the Unicorn and Yeti early reader series.

Hazel Quintanilla lives in Guatemala. Hazel always knew she wanted to be an artist. When she was a kid, she carried a pencil and a notebook everywhere.

Hazel illustrates children's books, magazines, and games! And she has a secret: Unicorn and Yeti remind Hazel of her sister and brother. Her siblings are silly, funny, and quirky — just like Unicorn and Yeti!

YOU CAN DRAW YETI IN A FANCY SUIT!

1. Draw one large oval for Yeti's body. Draw a circle for his face. (Draw lightly with a pencil! You will erase as you go.)

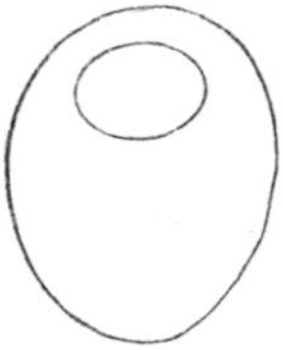

2. Add two ovals for Yeti's arms. One arm is bent, so draw a swoop to connect that arm to Yeti's body! Then add two soft triangles for his legs.

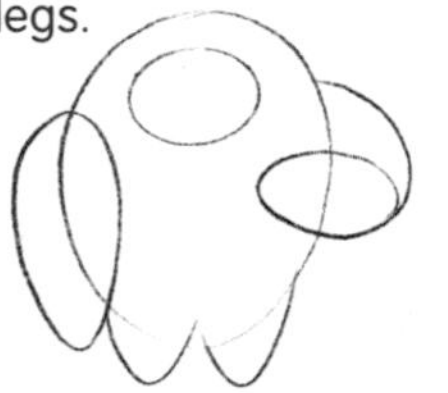

3. Draw fur on Yeti's forehead and on the top of his head. Give him eyebrows, a nose, and a smile!

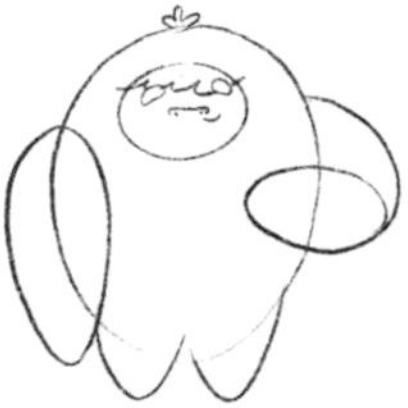

4. Draw the outline of Yeti's jacket and pants. (Erase some body lines as you go.) Give him ovals for hands and add two furry feet!

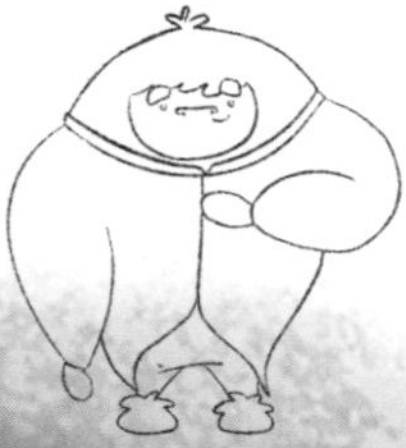

5. Add details—such as buttons, stripes, fancy shoulder fringe, and rosy cheeks!

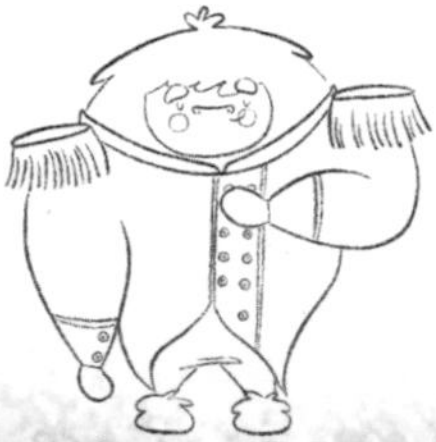

6. Color in your drawing!

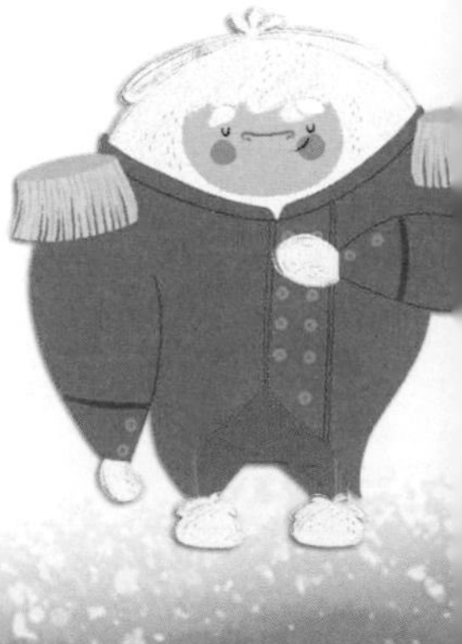

WHAT'S YOUR STORY?

Unicorn and Yeti dress up for a fancy tea party! Imagine **you** get to dress up and drink tea with them. What would you wear? How fancy would you be? Write and draw your story!

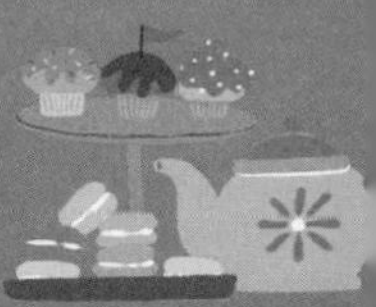

scholastic.com/acorn

Christy's Chance isn't an ordinary story and you don't read it like an ordinary book. Here's how it works.

In the beginning, you meet the characters and learn a little about them — who they are, where they live, what they do. After that, the story depends on you. When Christy and her friend Steven have a decision to make, you get to make it. Your choice will take you to a different part of the book, where you'll discover what happened as a result of your decision. As you read you'll continue to make choices until you come to the end. When you finish one story go back, make different choices. There are many stories in the same book. What happens to Christy and Steven is up to you. You make the story happen — *it's your choice.*

IT'S YOUR CHOICE
Nonfiction Series
by David R. Stronck

Alcohol: The Real Story
Tobacco: The Real Story
Marijuana: The Real Story

IT'S YOUR CHOICE
Fiction Series
By Christine DeVault and Bryan Strong

Serena's Secret (Alcohol)
Danny's Dilemma (Tobacco)
Christy's Chance (Marijuana)

IT'S YOUR CHOICE
Teacher's Guides
are also available.

Attention: Schools and Organizations

IT'S YOUR CHOICE books are available at quantity discounts
with bulk purchase for education, business or promotional use.
For information, please write or call:

Special Sales Department
Network Publications
A Division of ETR Associates
P.O. Box 1830
Santa Cruz, CA 95061-1830
1-(800) 321-4407

Christy's Chance

Christine DeVault/Bryan Strong

Illustrated by Robert Ransom

Network Publications
a division of ETR Associates
Santa Cruz, CA
1987

Library of Congress Cataloging-in-Publication Data

DeVault, Christine.
  Christy's chance.

  (It's your choice)
  Summary: The reader tries to help Christy
make decisions about using marijuana and
shares with her the consequences of each decision.
  1. Plot-your-own stories. 2. Marijuana—
Juvenile fiction. [1. Marijuana—Fiction.
2. Drug abuse—Fiction. 3. Conduct of
life—Fiction. 4. Plot-your-own stories] I.
Strong, Bryan. II. Ransom, Robert, 1962- ,
ill. III. Title. IV. Series.
PZ7.D496Ch 1987   [Fic]   87-18542

ISBN 0-941816-33-8 (pbk.)

Christy's Chance

Christy Jacobs stretched, sighed, and rolled over onto her stomach. Propping herself on her elbows, she reached up for the eject button of the cassette player. She removed the tape and rummaged in her bag for another one.

"How about something mellow?" Christy's cousin Heather asked.

"Mmm, okay...." She rummaged some more. "Ah! Here it is."

As the guitar's soothing sound washed over her, Christy stretched out once more on the warm, sandy shore of Harmony Lake. She could feel the sun's heat sinking into every part of her body. She felt relaxed and drowsy. It was wonderful.

*　*　*

She'd only been at the lake for a week, but so far it was the best summer vacation she'd ever had. Heather and Christy's mothers were sisters. Aunt Sylvia and Uncle Roger Kline and their three children, Heather, Jonathan, and Carrie, had moved to Harmony Lake four years earlier.

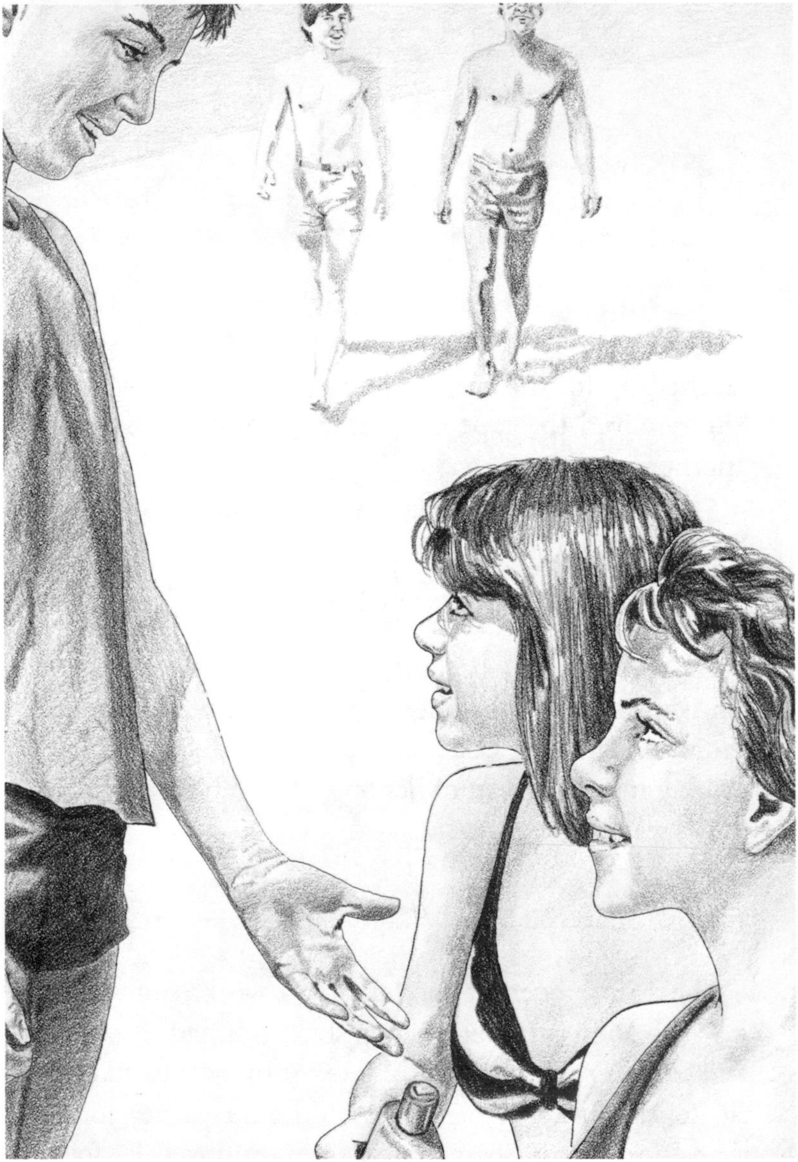

"Need some help with the suntan oil, girls?" asked Andrew.

Before that, the families had lived near each other and spent a lot of time together. Christy and Heather felt like sisters. Now they only saw each other once or twice a year although they wrote frequently.

Five more weeks of heaven, thought Christy. Five more weeks of swimming, boating, fishing, sunbathing, talking, and laughing with Heather and her friends. And five more weeks of checking out all the guys.

Christy sighed again. The only thing I wish, she thought, is that one of those guys would take a little more interest in me. Especially Eric Brodsky.

She pushed herself up, fluffed out her hair, and reached for the suntan oil. And I also wish, she thought, that I could lose ten pounds. "Disgusting," she remarked, rubbing the oil onto her well-rounded legs.

"You say something?" Heather asked.

"No. This black and white bathing suit makes me look like a penguin," said Christy.

"Don't be ridiculous. It looks great on you. At least your ribs don't stick out like mine."

"Heather, you're crazy. You should be a model. I'd give anything for your legs."

"Could you give me the suntan oil then?" Heather asked.

"Need some help with that, girls?" It was Andrew Vitale, who was, in Heather's opinion, "a total fox."

With him were Todd Johnson, who was very dark and very handsome, and (oh help, thought Christy) Eric Brodsky.

"No, thanks. We can manage," said Heather. But she smiled a little and winked at Christy.

"C'mon, let me help," said Andrew. He plopped himself in the sand next to Heather and took the suntan oil bottle from her. She held her long hair up off her neck while Andrew rubbed the oil onto her back and shoulders.

She looks like the cat that ate the cream, thought Christy. Todd and Eric nervously shuffled their feet in the sand. "You guys want something to drink?" she offered, reaching for the ice chest.

"Uh, sure. Thanks," said Todd, sitting down next to her. Eric sat down too. Christy passed around the cold cans of soda.

"That's great, thanks," said Eric, appearing to notice Christy for the first time. He smiled.

"Sure," she said. She tried not to stare at his eyelashes and to think of something clever to say.

"Is that your tape?" Todd asked.

"Yeah."

"It's far out. You got any others?"

Christy dumped the tapes from her bag onto her beach towel. Eric and Todd sifted through them. They talked about the groups they liked. Christy and Todd, who was also a summer visitor to the lake, talked about the concerts they'd been to.

"You guys are lucky," said Eric. "Nothing exciting ever happens around Harmony Lake, population 962."

"Hey, that reminds me," broke in Andrew, "something is gonna happen here. My mom got a call from Richard Hartman. You know, the movie director. They're gonna make a movie here and they needed a bunch of rooms for the crew and the stars and everybody."

"Oh, Andrew, I'm sure. Richard Hartman called your mom?" said Heather.

"Well, *he* didn't exactly call. It was his secretary or somebody. Anyway they're coming next week. They reserved all the rooms in our hotel."

"Big deal. All eight rooms," said Eric.

"Plus," Andrew continued, "Mom called around and booked more rooms for them at the motels and space at Avila's trailer park. She's also asking if anyone wants to rent out rooms in their homes."

"How long are they staying?"

"About two or three weeks, I guess."

"So do you know who's gonna be in the movie?" Heather asked.

Andrew smiled. "Uh huh."

"Well?" she demanded.

"What'll you give me if I tell you?"

"You better tell me or you'll get a knuckle taco," said Heather. She put her fist next to his nose.

"Okay. It's Sean Harris."

Christy and Heather let out a piercing shriek. "Sean Harris? You mean the real Sean Harris?"

"Oh, I'm gonna die!" exclaimed Christy. "He can stay in our room, can't he, Heather?"

"Sorry. He's staying at the hotel." Andrew said.

"Wow. Do you know who else is gonna be in it?"

"Josie Lansing, they said. That's all I know about."

"She's a babe!" said Eric.

The group sat silently for a minute, while the impact of the news sank in. Then Todd jumped up. "I don't know about you all, but I'm going for a swim."

Andrew got up too. "You coming, Heather?"

Christy and Eric were left alone. "You want to listen to another tape?" Christy asked.

"Okay."

Christy changed the cassette and lay down on her stomach. "You want some oil on your back?" Eric asked.

"Sure, thanks." She closed her eyes. Heaven!

*   *   *

At the dinner table that night, Christy and Heather talked excitedly of the upcoming moviemaking.

"Hmm," said Uncle Roger. "I wonder why I didn't

hear about this sooner." He was the editor of the local newspaper, the *Harmony Advocate,* and also ran a small printing business. Usually he knew everything that was happening in Harmony Lake.

"Oh, Daddy!" exclaimed Heather. "Just think—you can interview Sean Harris and Josie Lansing."

"Maybe we can hold the tape recorder?" Christy suggested.

"Settle down, girls," said Aunt Sylvia. "We don't even know if all these Hollywood people will want to associate with us ordinary folks."

"This event is certainly going to have the town in an uproar," said Uncle Roger.

Jonathan, who was sixteen and had a weird sense of humor, was humming scary background music. "Oooeee-ooo...it's *Invaders from Hollywood.*"

"Is it gonna be a spooky movie?" eight-year-old Carrie wanted to know.

"We don't know," said Aunt Sylvia. "We'll have to wait and see."

* * *

The following Friday evening was Teen Night at Harmony Lake Recreation Hall. Some of the kids went to dance to the records and tapes they played. Some went to play pool and pinball. A few went to drink beer and

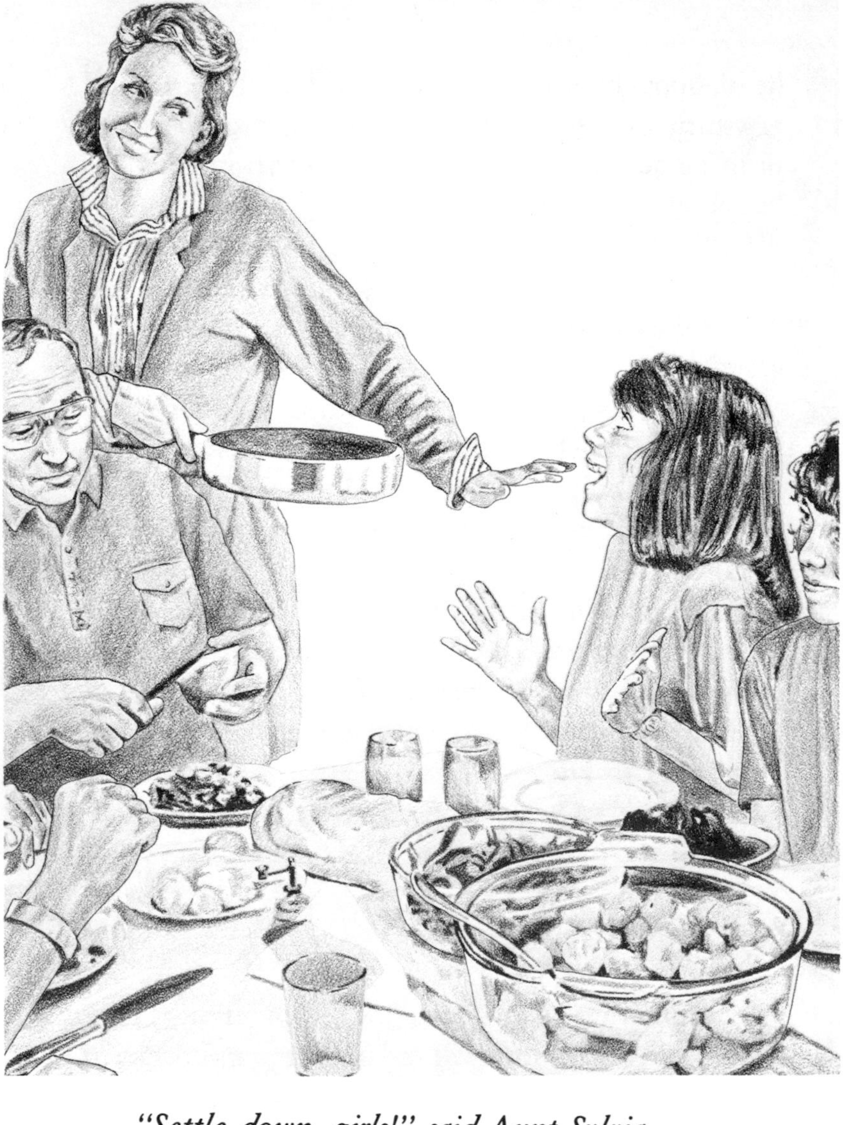

"Settle down, girls!" said Aunt Sylvia.

smoke pot in the rec hall parking lot.

Nearly everyone went to check out the other kids. They wanted to find out who was vacationing at the lake. The year-round residents also checked out each other. It was important to keep up on who was going with whom and who was available. Summer romances were frequent.

Jon, Heather, and Christy walked over to the rec hall around 8:00. Jon spotted his friends Steve Parker and Todd Johnson playing pool. Amy Tanaka was watching them. He immediately went to join them.

"That's the last we'll see of him," said Heather. "He'll follow Amy around all night."

The girls wandered around inside the hall for a while. Music was blaring but no one was dancing. A few people were sitting on benches in the dimly-lit corners of the room, but the girls didn't see anyone they knew.

"Mostly summer people, I guess," said Heather. "Let's check outside."

They went out the side door into the parking lot. There was just one light in the lot, near the rec hall door. The kids who brought cars usually parked as far as possible from the light.

From time to time someone from the recreation staff would come out to the cars to see what was happening. Usually the police came by once a night too. The kids who didn't want to be seen were pretty careful.

Sometimes they drove out to a spot next to the lake called Hawk's Point. Heather and Christy weren't allowed to go anywhere by car without permission. They'd never been to Hawk's Point.

A group of kids stood in the lighted area outside the door. There were two girls and two guys. "Wait a minute," whispered Heather, grabbing Christy's arm. "It's Andrew and Eric. Let's see what they do."

They didn't seem to be doing very much except talking and laughing. Then Eric put his arm around one of the girls. "Drat!" muttered Christy.

Heather pulled her forward. "C'mon!"

"Heather! Hi!" said Andrew. "Hi, Christy."

Christy smiled back and said hello to Eric. She didn't know the two girls. She didn't want to know the one that was hanging all over Eric.

"Uh, Heather and Christy, this is...uh...Megan and Jennifer," Andrew said. "They're here for the summer. We were just telling them what there is to do in Harmony Lake."

"More like what there *isn't* to do," said Eric. Eric's "friend" Megan giggled.

She's got shifty eyes, Christy thought. She gave Megan her phoniest smile. Jennifer looks nice though, she thought.

"You guys want to walk over to Tom Rice's car with us?" Andrew asked. "We've got a little business to do."

"Sure," said Heather.

Christy followed, a little behind the others. She wished she had the nerve to go back into the hall and hang out with Jon. It was bugging her to see Eric and Megan together. And Heather had lost all interest in her cousin now that she was with Andrew.

Eric and Andrew leaned into the window on the driver's side of Tom Rice's '55 Chevy.

Jennifer turned to Christy. "Nice car," she said.

"For sure," Christy agreed.

"Are you from around here?" Jennifer asked.

"No, I'm from Rosemont. I'm staying at my cousin's this summer," Christy said.

"Rosemont! That's amazing!" It turned out that Jennifer lived near Christy's home town. They talked for a few minutes and discovered they knew some of the same people.

Eric and Andrew had finished talking to Tom. They looked pleased. "You want to go with us out to Hawk's Point?" Eric asked. "Tom'll drive."

Christy looked at Heather. Heather looked confused.

I'll bet she really wants to go, thought Christy. And I *can't* let her go without me. But what if Aunt Sylvia and Uncle Roger find out...? Plus who wants to watch Eric flirt with Miss Shifty Eyes?

"If we don't stay too long...." Heather said. "Okay, Christy?"

Then Eric smiled at her. "C'mon, Chris. I got something special."

Andrew opened the car door. Oh shoot, thought Christy. What should I do?

What did Christy do?

Choice A
If you think Christy got into the car,
turn to page 17.

Choice B
If you think Christy did not *get into the car,*
turn to page 13.

Christy's mind was racing. She really wanted more time to think. "Can you wait a minute?" she asked. "I've got to go to the restroom. *Now.*"

"Oh, all right," grumbled Andrew. "But hurry up."

"Okay. Heather, c'mon with me." The two girls ran across the lot and into the rec hall.

Once inside, Christy turned to Heather and grabbed her arm. "You don't really think we should go, do you?"

"Well, I want to be with Andrew."

"But Heather, your folks will kill us if they find out."

"It'll just be for a little while, Christy. They won't find out."

"Oh, sure. You're always saying there're no secrets in a small town."

"Well, I don't think they'll find out. Anyway, don't you want a chance to get to know Eric better?" asked Heather.

"Oh, right. With that scuzzy Megan crawling all over him," replied Christy in disgust.

"He doesn't really like her, I can tell. I think he's interested in you. He wants you to come."

Christy sighed. "He sure is cute." He did seem kind of interested, she thought. "By the way," she said, "do you know what he was talking about—what 'something special' is supposed to mean?"

Heather looked uncomfortable. She hesitated. "Um...well...y'see, they're getting some pot from Tom."

Christy stared at her cousin. "Heather, are you kidding?"

"No. What's the big deal anyway?"

"Oh, no big deal! First you want to get in some guy's car and drive out to the boonies and risk getting murdered by your parents as a result. Then you want to get all messed up on pot. Pot's just as bad for you as beer. And it is *illegal,* you know. But it's no big deal," she added sarcastically.

"C'mon, Christy, haven't you ever tried it?"

"No, actually, I haven't. And I don't care to.... I didn't know you smoked it."

"Well, I've just tried it a couple of times. Nothing really happened. C'mon, Christy. It's not like you to be so nervous."

"Oh, Heather. It just sounds too risky, that's all." Christy felt like crying. She loved Heather and hated having bad feelings between them. She really didn't want to let Heather go without her. But she was beginning to think maybe she should.

"Well, I'm going," said Heather. "With or without you."

She turned and walked right into her older brother. "Where're you going 'with or without' Christy?" Jon asked.

"Oh, just somewhere. It's no big deal, Jon," said Heather guiltily.

"It looks like it's a big deal to Christy," Jon said, looking closely at Christy. "Anyway, Christy, I'm supposed to ask you if you want to play pool with me and Amy and Steve."

"You're supposed to ask me?" Christy said. "Who says?"

"You met Steve before, right? He...uh...likes you. He's kind of shy, so I told him I'd get you to come over."

Christy looked over at the pool table. Steve was bent over his cue, concentrating on a difficult shot. He missed. He straightened up and glanced over at Christy. He shrugged and grinned. Christy felt herself beginning to blush.

What's wrong with me? she thought. I don't even know the guy. I only met him once for about five minutes. She remembered that he had seemed friendly and kind of funny in a quiet way. He looked nice, with his reddish hair and freckles and easy smile. Not handsome like Eric, but nice all the same.

"Well, I'm going outside," said Heather. "Bye, Christy."

"Just a second," said Christy. "Give me a chance to think."

I guess Heather's going whether I do or not, she thought. I should probably go to make sure she doesn't do anything stupid. And maybe Eric really does like me. Anyway, I wouldn't have to smoke anything.

Then she thought about Steve. She wished she could be two places at the same time.

What did Christy do?

Choice A
If you think Christy decided to go with Heather,
turn to page 17.

Choice B
If you think Christy decided to stay and play pool with Jon, Amy, and Steve,
turn to page 25.

Tom pulled the Chevy off the road at Hawk's Point. Christy scrambled out of the back seat as quickly as she could. The moon was bright. She found the path to a large boulder that overlooked the peaceful lake. She sat down with a sigh and stared out at the pattern of moonlight on the lake's surface.

Being wedged in the back seat with Andrew, Heather, and Jennifer had been bad enough. But watching Megan flirt with Eric and Tom was even worse. Heather had Andrew, Megan had Eric and Tom. Who did she have? Jennifer!

Poor Jennifer, thought Christy. I shouldn't have left her back there. She was thinking she'd go back and see if Jennifer was okay when she heard footsteps on the path.

"Is anything wrong?"

"Eric! No...I just wanted to look at the view." It's better than the view back in the car, she thought.

"Is there room for one more?" he asked.

"Oh...sure." She scooted over on the boulder. "What happened to your friend?"

"Friend? You mean Megan? Oh...she's back there."

Hmm, thought Christy. She probably decided to be with Tom. She gave Eric a sidelong glance.

"What's the matter?" he asked.

"Nothin'. " Then she added, "Tough luck."

He gave a short laugh. "I didn't really like her any-

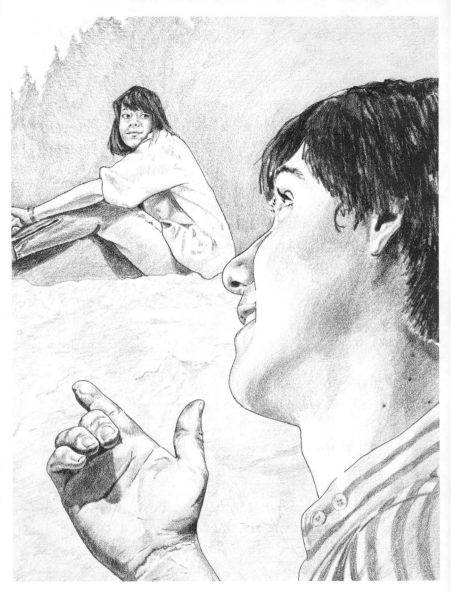

"Is there room for one more, Christy?" Eric asked.

way...Listen..." He reached into his pocket. "You want to share this with me?"

It was the first time Christy had seen a joint. She'd heard a lot about marijuana, but none of her friends back home used it.

"It's pretty good for local weed," Eric was saying.

"Local weed?"

"Yeah. They grow it in the hills around here." Eric lit the cigarette and inhaled deeply. He held it out to her.

She took it awkwardly. Now what do I do? she wondered. I probably won't turn into a green monster or anything if I try it. And if I don't, he'll think I'm chicken and boring. But what if something bad happens? What if I lose control of myself and start acting weird? What if I freak out? What if someone—like Uncle Roger—finds out?

"Hey...haven't you smoked grass before?"

"Uh, well...no, actually." This is so embarrassing, she thought.

"It's easy. Go on. You'll like it." He gave her an encouraging smile.

He's really cute, she thought. And he does seem to like me after all.

"C'mon, Christy. You're not chicken, are you?"

What did Christy do?

Choice A
If you think Christy decided to try marijuana,
turn to page 21.

Choice B
If you think Christy decided not *to smoke marijuana,*
turn to page 22.

Christy put the slim cigarette to her lips. When she inhaled, the smoke stung her throat and lungs. She coughed.

"Hey, take it easy," said Eric. He took the joint from her. "Don't try to get too much."

She tried again. This time she didn't choke.

They smoked a little more. Then Eric carefully stubbed out the cigarette and returned it to his pocket.

"Pretty good weed, huh?" he asked.

Christy smiled at him. She didn't really feel much of anything. If my friends could see me now, she thought. Sitting in this romantic spot with this cute guy. She giggled.

"What's so funny?" Eric asked, slipping his arm around her.

"Nothing. I just...why...I just...forgot what I was going to say." She suddenly had an uncomfortable, light-headed feeling.

"Hey! You guys!" Christy jumped. It was Heather. "We'd better get back," she said. "We've got to be in by midnight."

Christy sighed. Eric took her hand and helped her down. The ride back to town wasn't uncomfortable at all. This time Jennifer sat in front next to Megan, and Christy was quite happily wedged between Heather and Eric.

Turn to page 28.

"Cluck, cluck," said Christy. "Actually, I guess I am. I just hate the idea of black, sticky smoke inside my cute, pink lungs. I've heard pot is just as bad for your lungs as tobacco." She handed the slim cigarette back to him.

Eric gave a short laugh. "Okay," he said. "Whatever."

He smoked some more of the joint. Then he stubbed out the end and carefully put it back into his pocket.

"You're lucky to live out here," Christy said. She hoped he wouldn't think she was a total idiot.

"Yeah, I guess. Except that nothin' ever happens. As soon as I finish school, I'm splitting."

"How much more school do you have?"

"Two years. How about you?" he asked.

"Three."

Eric nodded. He stared out over the lake. "Well," he said, standing up, "I'm gonna go see what they're doin'. You want to come?" He held out his hand.

Christy took it and they walked back to the car. Jennifer was sitting on a fallen log. She was pushing rocks around with her toe. "The lovebirds are all inside," she said, nodding toward the car. She looked disgusted.

I know just how she feels, thought Christy. She sat down next to Jennifer.

"Where'd you go, anyway?" Jennifer asked.

"There's an overlook up the path there. It's a great view. I was going to come back and see if you wanted to go out there. But then Eric came over...."

"Were you smoking pot?" Jennifer asked.

"Uh...no, actually. *I* wasn't."

"Oh. I was just wondering."

"Did *you* have some?" asked Christy.

"Just one hit. Then I came out here."

Christy and Jennifer sat and talked. Eric wandered around. He went back to the overlook and threw rocks into the lake. Then he went back to the car and tapped on the window.

"We should probably get going," Christy said. "If we're not home by midnight, Heather's dad will turn us into pumpkins."

Turn to page 37.

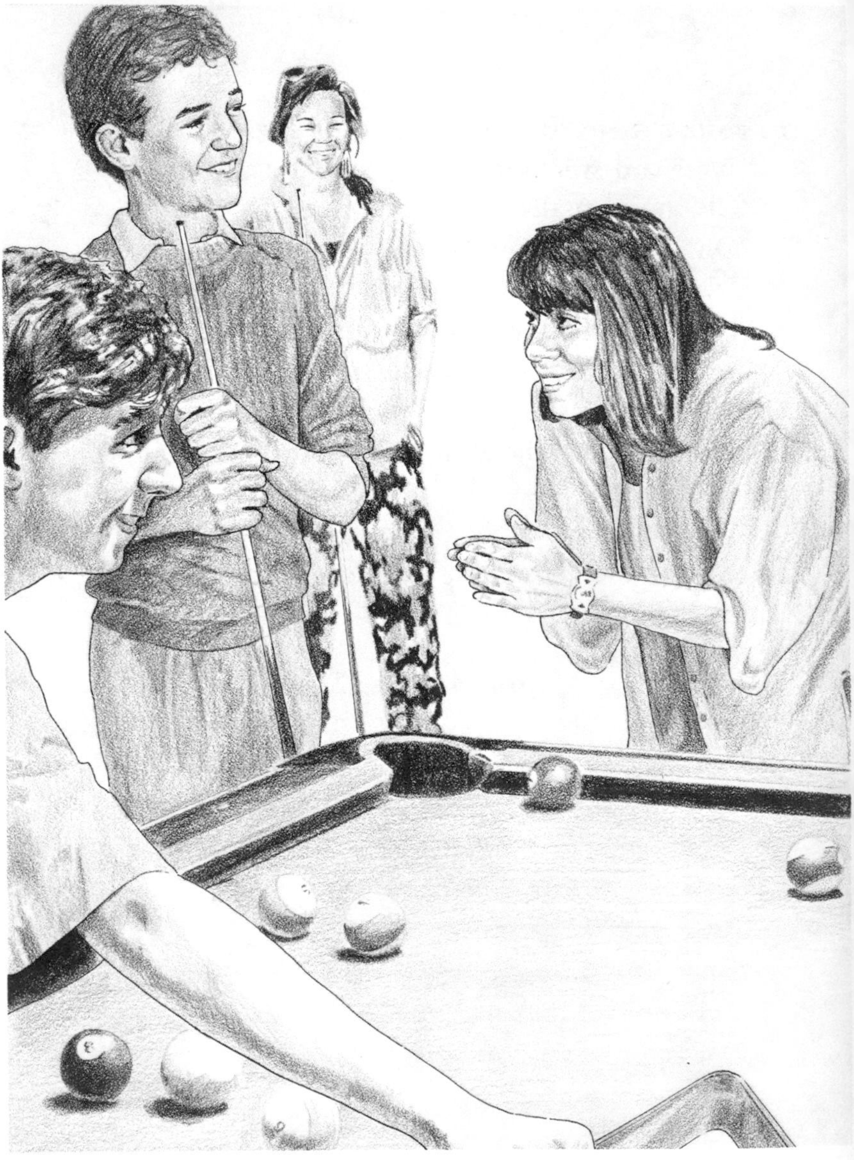

"Okay," Christy said to Steve, "rack 'em up!"

Christy glanced over at Steve again. He was holding the pool cue out in front of him with the point toward his stomach. He gave her a pleading look.

"What in the world is he doing?" she asked.

Jon looked over. "Oh, that's just his way of saying he's dying to meet you."

"Oh...okay," she laughed, shaking her head. "I can't resist." She turned to Heather. "I'll just walk over to the door with you."

When they were out of earshot from Jon, she said, "Tell them I'm not feeling so good, okay? And be careful! Don't do anything stupid."

"Don't worry. I'll see you later." Heather slipped out into the night.

Christy walked over to the pool table. "Okay," she said, rubbing her hands together, "rack 'em up." She grinned at Steve as she selected a cue.

"Uh oh," he said. "Are you a pro at this?"

"Not exactly. But my stepdad is. And he taught me everything he knows. Who's playing who?"

Amy and Christy then proceeded to beat the pants off the guys.

Later on the four of them sat around a table in a booth at Pizza Heaven. They were laughing hysterically about the pool game.

"I can't get over you," Steve said to Christy. "I mean you look so sweet and innocent. And then you just turn into this...this mad fiend. You murdered us."

"Amy did her part, too," said Christy generously.

"Oh, sure," said Amy. "I barely had a chance to make a shot. You're totally awesome."

"It's awesome how you can eat so much pizza," said Christy, eyeing Amy's slim figure. "I hate you."

"Myself," said Steve, sliding closer to Christy, "I like a girl I can get a good grip on." He waggled his fingers at Christy and cackled like a mad scientist.

"You're crazy," she said. But she didn't move away.

"Christy," Jon said, "where'd Heather go anyway?"

Christy gave him a guilty look. "You should ask her yourself, okay? It's nothing bad, really. I just think it should be left up to her."

Jon shook his head. "I just hope she doesn't do anything dumb."

"She won't," said Christy.

"I hope not. I'm gonna walk Amy home now. I'll see you guys later."

"I'd better get home too," said Christy.

A few minutes before midnight Christy and Steve were sitting on a low wall at the edge of the Kline's front yard. They had been talking nonstop. "I've got to go in now, I'm afraid," Christy said. "Heather or no Heather."

Tom's Chevy rounded the corner then. Christy sighed with relief. She waved toward the car as it stopped.

Andrew helped Heather out. Then Jennifer put her head out and waved. That looks like Megan next to Tom, Christy thought. I wonder where Eric is.

"You had me worried for a minute there," Christy told her cousin.

"I told you I'd be all right, silly. We'd better get in."

Christy turned to Steve. "Well, it's been real fun." He really does have a cute face, she thought. Nice eyes.

Steve smiled. He gave her nose a gentle tweak. "I'll see you soon, okay?"

"How soon?"

"How about tomorrow?"

"Okay. I guess I can wait that long."

She turned and followed Heather into the house.

Turn to page 37.

The following week was one of growing excitement for the normally quiet town of Harmony Lake. The crew that would be filming *Last Chance Lake* arrived and began to work.

The location director took tours by car and boat looking for the best places to shoot the lake scenes. She talked to various business people and homeowners about using their work places or houses for other scenes.

The casting director, Lois Kahn, signed up people to be extras. Most of the extras just had to be in the background while the principal actors performed. But there were a few speaking parts available. Christy felt like dying of shock and happiness when Lois asked her if she'd like to have a few lines to speak.

"We'll do some test shots tomorrow just to make sure you can handle the part," Lois said. "Don't worry. You won't have to memorize anything yet. Can you meet me at the main dock tomorrow morning at 10:00?"

"I'll be there," said Christy.

*   *   *

The following morning, Christy and Heather were at the boat dock at 9:30. They watched the film crew busily preparing for the day's work. Steve Parker, Todd, Amy, and some of the other kids were there too.

Richard Hartman, the director, had arrived the night

before. Now he was out on the dock talking to a woman who was setting up microphones. "He's so short," said Heather. "I thought he'd be taller."

"Yeah, and he's getting bald too," giggled Amy.

"Well, why not?" exclaimed Christy. "These people are human too. They're not any different from anyone else."

"Just wait till Sean Harris gets here," said Heather. "Then see how cool she acts."

Lois Kahn arrived then. She explained the test shots they would be making. Then they got to work.

After Christy read her lines in front of the camera a few times, Lois told her she'd done fine. She had the part for sure. Now she had to memorize her lines. They would shoot her scene some time the following week.

Christy grabbed Heather and they jumped up and down. "Let's celebrate, Heath. I'll buy us lunch at Pizza Heaven."

As the two girls were finishing the last bits of their pepperoni and olive combo, Andrew and Eric walked in. Christy hadn't seen much of Eric since the previous weekend. She wasn't sure how he felt about her even though Heather kept saying, "I know he really likes you. He's just shy." Moody is more like it, Christy thought.

"Hey, did you hear?" Heather called out to the guys. "Christy's gonna be a movie star."

Andrew and Eric ordered their pizza and joined the girls. Christy scooted over to make room for Eric. He congratulated her on her part.

"Thanks," she said. "It's not much though. All I have to say is: 'I saw her last night at Tiny's Grill. She was with some old guy. I thought maybe he was her father.'"

"Pretty good," said Eric. "Look out, Hollywood."

"So where've you been this past week?" Christy asked.

"Workin'. I got a job clearing some land over on the other side. They're gonna film a lot of the movie over there. It'll be the camp where the bad guys are holding Josie Lansing."

"Wow! That sounds neat." said Christy.

"It's okay. It's hard work, but I've met some cool guys from the movie crew. I've been thinking about going to Los Angeles when I get out of school. Or maybe sooner."

The boys' pizza arrived then and was quickly taken care of. "Should I tell the girls?" Andrew asked Eric, between mouthfuls of sausage and mozzarella cheese.

"Tell us what?" cried Christy and Heather.

"Oh...something about Sean Harris.... Now girls, calm down."

"Do you want to murder him, Heather, or can I?" Christy asked.

"Let's do it together. I'll hold. You tickle."

"All right, all right. I give!" gasped Andrew as the girls pounced on him.

He told them that Sean Harris was due to arrive at his family's hotel the next day, along with several other members of the cast of *Last Chance Lake*.

"You'll help us find a way to meet him, won't you, Andrew, honey, sweetie, dearest?" said Heather, batting her eyelashes.

"We'll see," said Andrew. "No more tickling."

"Well," said Eric. "I've gotta be going. I'm going over to Conrad's Garage to see Tom." He turned to Christy. "You want to come?"

"Oh...sure. Where are you gonna be later, Heather?"

"At the main beach prob'ly. Unless I take the rowboat out," said Heather.

"Okay. I'll find you. Later, Andrew," said Christy. "See you."

* * *

At the garage they found Tom Rice, or rather, Tom Rice's feet, sticking out from under a battered pickup truck.

"Hey, Tom," Eric called, "can I talk to you a minute?"

A greasy Tom emerged. He wiped his hands on a dirty rag and nodded at Christy. Then he and Eric walked over to the edge of the parking lot. They talked

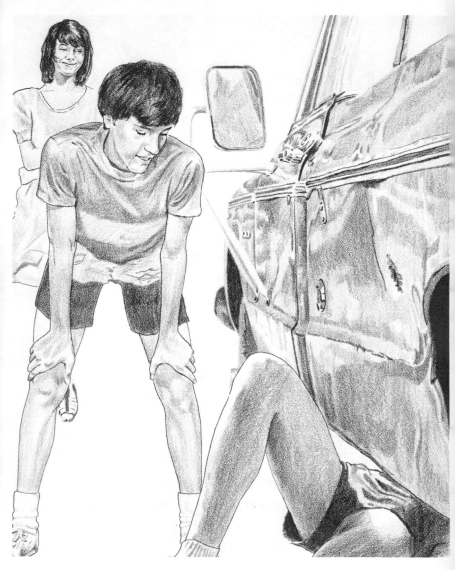

Christy and Eric found Tom Rice at the garage. "Hey, Tom," Eric said, "can I talk to you a minute?"

softly for a few minutes.

Hmm, thought Christy. I bet I know what that's about. Probably a drug deal. She went to the water fountain and got a drink. Then she leaned against the wall of the building and waited. Sure enough, she thought, as Eric slipped Tom some money.

She looked around uneasily. I'd leave right this minute, she thought, except that would be the end of me and Eric.

Then Eric came toward her. "Okay," he said, "All done. What you want to do now?"

"It's so hot. I was gonna go back to the house and get my suit on and then go to the beach."

"Mind if I join you?"

"Of course not." Oh far out! He really does like me, she thought.

The rest of the afternoon sailed by. Christy and Eric lay side by side on the beach. Then they took the row-boat out to tiny Shadow Island in the center of the lake.

The beach on the island was too rocky for swimming, but the island was beautiful and very peaceful. They sat on the rocky shore and looked back at the main-land. "It could be a million miles away," said Christy. "Without a boat there's no way to communicate. Even though you can see the people on the shore."

"Yeah. Like a silent—well, almost-silent—movie," said Eric. He reached into the pouch of his sweatshirt and took out a small plastic bag. "The perfect treat to go with our movie." He took a cigarette paper from the bag and sprinkled some marijuana leaves into it. Then he expertly rolled it up and lit it.

Well, thought Christy, as she took the joint from him, I smoked it before. I guess it won't hurt to try it again.

This time, though, she thought she could feel the effects more strongly. As she and Eric watched the tiny figures across the lake perform in their "movie," she found herself laughing helplessly.

"Look," she giggled, "There's Heather... No, over there—the speck with the red bikini. Yes, there. Okay, now, the speck with the white trunks—that's Andrew. See, he just picked her up. He's going to throw her back in the water. He says, 'This isn't the kind of fish I was looking for.' "

Christy and Eric continued to make up lines for the "characters" on the opposite shore. Christy kept starting to talk and then forgetting what she wanted to say.

Then she started to feel uncomfortable. Her heart was racing. She found herself worrying about what Eric might be thinking about her. She wanted to be back home, among familiar faces. "I think I'd better be getting back," she said.

"Okay," said Eric. "Whatever you say."

As they rowed back, Christy started to feel calmer.

"Listen," Eric said suddenly, "could you do me a favor?"

"Sure. What?"

"I need you to take something over to Avila's trailer park for me. Later on tonight," he said.

"Uh, okay. What is it? Why can't you take it?"

"Well, Kim Avila's dad doesn't like me. He thinks I'm a bad influence on her. Anyway, I have to get a package over to a guy from the movie crew."

"You mean *pot*?" Christy asked.

"Yeah. Of course. Is that a big deal?"

"You want *me* to deliver *drugs* for you?"

"Forget it then, Christy. I thought you were cool."

"Eric." Christy sat up straight and reached toward him. "I'm not saying I won't, okay? I was just kind of surprised." She touched his arm gently.

She tried to think clearly. It was obviously important to him. And she didn't want to let him down. But what if she got caught? What if her family found out? What if the police...?

"There's no danger at all, Christy. Otherwise I wouldn't ask you. But I really can't go over there myself. It'll only take a few minutes. Then we can go do something afterwards." He smiled and squeezed her hand.

Am I being used? she wondered. Does he really like me or is he just looking for someone to do his dirty work? How will I feel about myself if I do this?

What did Christy do?

Choice A
*If you think Christy decided to deliver
the marijuana for Eric,*
turn to page 51.

Choice B
If you think Christy decided not *to
deliver the marijuana,*
turn to page 48.

The following week was one of growing excitement for the normally quiet town of Harmony Lake. The crew that would be filming *Last Chance Lake* arrived and began to work.

The location director took tours by car and boat looking for the best places to shoot the lake scenes. She talked to various business people and homeowners about using their work places or houses for other scenes.

The casting director, Lois Kahn, signed up people to be extras. Most of the extras just had to be in the background as the principal actors performed. But there were a few speaking parts available. Christy felt like dying of shock and happiness when Lois asked her if she'd like to have a few lines to speak. "We'll do some test shots tomorrow just to make sure you can handle the part," Lois said.

* * *

The following morning, Christy and Heather were at the main boat dock at 9:30. They watched the film crew busily preparing for the day's work. Steve, Todd, Amy, and some of the other kids were there too.

After Christy read her lines in front of the camera a few times, Lois told her she'd done fine. She had the part for sure. Now she had to memorize her lines. They would shoot the scene some time the following week.

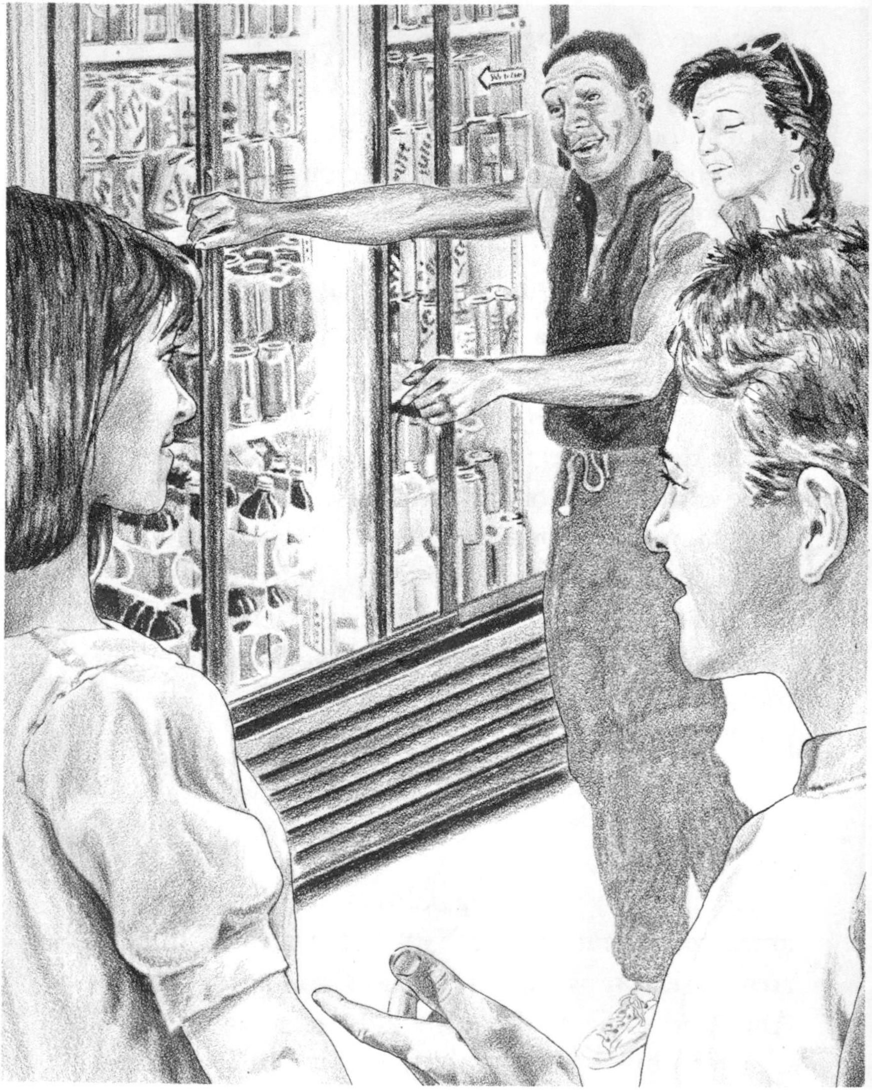

"The drinks are on me," said Todd. "What do you want?"

"Congratulations, Christy!" Steve hugged her and slapped her on the back. "Do you two want to come over to my house for lunch? We can barbeque some stuff."

"You go on," said Heather. "I'm gonna look for Andrew."

"If you find him, bring him over too," said Steve.

Christy and Steve, along with Todd and Amy, went into the grocery store to shop for their lunch. Todd had gotten a speaking part in the film too. "The drinks are on me," he said. "What kind of soda do you all want?"

"Let me buy the hamburger," said Christy. "Since I'm gonna be famous *and* rich soon."

When they got to Steve's house, Amy and Steve called a few more kids. Soon the hamburgers were sizzling and the party was in full swing.

After they had eaten, Christy and Steve stretched out on the grass in the back yard. "You doing anything later on?" he asked.

"It depends," Christy said with a sly grin. "What were you thinking?"

"Oh, I don't know. There might a be party over on Shadow Island tonight. I heard some of the movie crew talking about it. Last year we had some pretty good cook-outs over there."

"Mmm. That sounds like fun."

*   *   *

The evening was clear and warm. The smooth waters of the lake reflected the last red streaks of the dying sunset. Christy and Steve rowed over to Shadow Island with Amy and Jon. They could see bright, orange bonfires winking along the island's shore.

Motor boats weren't allowed on Harmony Lake. The only sounds were the splashing of oars and the laughter of the partygoers. Todd passed them, rowing at a lively pace. He had some people from the film crew in his boat. He and some of the other kids were doing a brisk business this evening. They were providing taxi service for the movie people.

"How much are you charging?" called Jon.

"A dollar per person," Todd called back. "*Each* way."

*   *   *

It looked like a good party. People were grilling fish and hamburgers over open coals. They were steaming a large kettle of clams.

Music filled the air. Several people had brought their tape players and they were all going at once. Someone else was playing a guitar. As it grew later, the party got louder. People danced and sang—mostly off-key.

Christy left Steve, who was having a friendly argument about baseball with one of the movie crew. She wandered happily through the boisterous crowd. She found her cousin Jon, sitting by himself. He was observing the action. She sat down next to him. "Where's Amy?"

"Uh...she had a little too much to drink. She's over in the woods being sick."

Christy was alarmed. "Is she all right?"

"Oh, yeah. I don't think she knew how much she was drinking," he said.

"I didn't know you drank." She was looking at the can of beer in Jon's hand.

"Just a little. This is just my second one. You want a beer?" Jon offered.

"No, thanks. I hate the taste."

Amy came back then. She looked a little pale but seemed to be feeling better. She leaned against Jon with her eyes closed.

They were soon joined by Steve and a couple of his new-found friends, Mark and Randy. Megan was there too, hanging on to Mark for dear life.

She sure gets around, thought Christy. She watched Megan carefully, making sure she didn't get too close to Steve. He seems to be awfully interested in her, Christy thought. He laughs at everything she says.

Randy moved closer to Christy. "You from around here?" he asked.

"I'm visiting my cousins for the summer." She took a good look at him then. Tall, blond, well-built. Not bad.

From the corner of her eye she could see Steve. He was still hanging on Megan's every word. She grinned up at Randy, deciding she'd like to get to know him better.

Christy told Randy about life at Harmony Lake. He told her a little about his life in Los Angeles. She asked him about Sean Harris but he didn't know much. Then he reached into his jacket and took out a small box. He took a slim cigarette from the box and lit it. He inhaled deeply and then offered it to Christy.

She shook her head and smiled. "Uh, no thanks. Not just now."

Randy leaned over and gave the joint to Mark. Mark inhaled and then passed it to Megan. She smoked a little and passed it to Steve. Steve took it but didn't smoke any. He got up and brought it back to Randy. He smiled at Christy. "How's it goin'?"

"Great," she said. She wondered if he had come over to protect her from Randy's influence. I can take care of myself, she thought.

When Randy held the joint out to her again, she took it. If Megan can do it, so can I, she thought. She put it to her lips and took a breath. The smoke burned her throat. She coughed.

"Easy does it," said Randy. "You okay?"

"Fine," she gasped.

Steve looked at her. He didn't say anything, but she thought he looked amused. When she smoked some more a little later on, he didn't look so amused.

As he watched Christy, Steve wondered what to do. He didn't think she should be smoking marijuana. If I tell her so, he thought, she'll probably be mad at me. But if I don't, she could be in big trouble. As he watched Christy, he realized how much she meant to him. It was really important not to lose her friendship.

What did Steve do?

Choice A
If you think Steve decided to tell Christy he didn't like her to smoke marijuana,
turn to page 44.

Choice B
If you think Steve decided not *to say anything about marijuana to Christy at this time,*
turn to page 46.

Steve cleared his throat. "Uh, Christy? You want to go for a walk? There're some neat rock formations over on the other side."

She looked at him for a moment. Then she stood up. "Sure." She turned to Randy. "See you later."

"It's kind of dark, don't you think?" she asked. They were following a path between the rocks and the forest's edge.

"I think there's enough moonlight. Your eyes will get used to it."

Away from the commotion of the party, the only sounds were the waves lapping against the rocks and the occasional call of a night bird.

They walked to a place where the rocks on the shore were formed into several small arches. "That's beautiful!" Christy exclaimed. "I wish I was six inches tall. I'd get a tiny boat and sail through the arches."

They sat down and watched the rocks and water in the moonlight. "Christy," Steve began, "I...I want you to know you're real special to me. *Very* special." He squeezed her hand.

She looked at him. He went on quickly. "So that's why I want to tell you I'm kinda worried about your smoking pot. I don't think it's a good idea."

She stared at him for a moment. Then she laughed. "Oh, that! I don't even like it! You don't have to worry. I'm not going to try it again."

He was puzzled. "Why'd you smoke it then?"

"I just wanted to get your attention."

"You didn't have to do that to get my attention!" Steve exclaimed.

"Well, you seemed awfully interested in Megan."

"That airhead? Give me a break. I have sort of, uh, sort of a *scientific* interest in her. I've been trying to figure out why she acts like she does."

"Oh, sure," said Christy. Then she started to giggle. She pictured Megan in a glass dish under a microscope. "You're weird," she said. "But you're cute."

"I know," said Steve. "But seriously, Christy, I'm glad you're here. I'm glad we met."

"Me too." She smiled at him and then looked out over the lake. This summer is turning out pretty well after all, she thought. Steve really seems to like me— just the way I am!

THE END

Steve got up and walked down to the water's edge. He kicked some rocks around for a while.

"Is something the matter?" It was Christy.

"Oh, hi! No...no, nothing's the matter."

"Oh. 'Cause you just disappeared all of a sudden."

"Well, it looked like you were busy."

"Busy?"

"You know. Smoking pot with that guy."

"Are you *jealous?*" she asked. As far as she knew, no one had ever been jealous over her before.

"No. I'm not jealous...well, maybe I am a little. Anyway, I don't like pot."

"Steve, there's nothing to be jealous about, believe me." She took his arm. "And I don't think that pot affects me. I don't really feel anything."

"But marijuana is a pretty strong drug, Christy. I've seen people get pretty spaced out on it. It makes them act stupid. Haven't you noticed that?"

"Noticed what?"

"See what I mean? You already lost track of what we were talking about," he said.

"Well, maybe I do feel a little strange. But it seems like everybody's smoking it. They'll think I'm weird if I don't."

"I don't smoke pot," Steve said. "And nobody gives me a hard time about it. Not that I'd care if they did."

"I feel like everybody's staring at me when they pass

it to me," Christy said.

"I figure they're probably too stoned to even notice what I'm doing," Steve replied. "I just take it and pass it on. Then I usually leave. Have you noticed how boring it gets around people that have been smoking pot?"

"Am I boring you?" she asked.

"Let's put it this way. I've seen you when you seemed smarter and a lot more alert," he replied.

"Thanks a lot." Now she felt like crying. She brushed at her eyes.

"Hey," Steve said softly. "I didn't mean to hurt your feelings. I wouldn't bother telling you the truth if I didn't care about you. How about if I row you home? No more heavy discussion, I promise."

"Okay." Christy felt confused. She was looking forward to going home and crawling into her warm, safe bed.

Turn to page 57.

They reached the dock then. Christy busied herself with tying up the boat while she tried to think of how to tell Eric what she'd decided. Just blurt it out, I guess, she thought.

"Eric, I just can't do it."

"Huh?"

"I can't make that delivery for you. I'm just too chicken."

Eric looked at her. He sighed and shook his head. "Whatever," he said with a shrug.

He looked so disappointed she almost changed her mind. But he didn't give her the chance. "Later," he said, turning and walking quickly up the dock.

Well! she thought. So he *was* just using me! Tears of outrage stung her eyes. She sat down on the dock's edge and put her feet in the cool water. She watched the spreading ripples. A few tears splashed among them. Stupid waste of time, she lamented. And I thought he liked me.

The afternoon was too beautiful for her to stay sad for long. Christy splashed some water on her face. At least I found out what Eric's really like, she thought. It's a good thing I didn't get more involved with him. And I'm glad I didn't let myself get talked into something I didn't think was right! She jumped up and headed home to help with dinner.

As she left the dock, she heard a shout. "Christy!

"Eric," Christy blurted out, "I just can't make that delivery for you."

Hey! Over here!" It was Steve Parker, her cousin Jon's friend. He greeted her like a long-lost pal. In the golden afternoon light, they walked slowly along the path back to town. They talked and laughed all the way. Christy was still chuckling when she joined Aunt Sylvia and Jon in the kitchen.

"Have a good day, honey?" her aunt inquired.

Christy thought for a moment. The day had certainly had its ups and downs. "Well," she said, "I guess it turned out pretty good after all." She thought about Steve and smiled to herself.

Turn to page 57.

"So what do you want me to do?" she asked.

"Can you meet me at Conrad's Garage at 8:00?" asked Eric. "And bring a purse or something."

"Okay," she said. "I'll be there."

*   *   *

At a quarter to eight, Christy left the house. Jon had gone over to Shadow Island to a big cook-out with some people from the movie crew. Heather and Andrew were going to the rec hall. Christy told them she was going to meet Eric. She said she would join them later on.

Christy sat on a low stone wall opposite Conrad's. A little after 8:00, Eric pulled up on his bike.

"Hi," he said, smiling. "I'm glad you showed."

She smiled uncertainly.

"I'll walk along with you a little way, okay?" he said.

She nodded. Eric reached into his jacket pocket and pulled out a brown paper sack. It was rolled up and taped securely. He slipped it into her shoulder bag.

As he pushed his bike along next to her, he told her where to take the package. "It's space 22. The guy's expecting you. His name is Art."

"So I just hand him the package and leave?"

"That's all."

"I hope I don't see anyone I know."

"Hey, don't worry so much. It'll be fine." He gave

her arm a squeeze and pedalled away.

Christy hurried down the road toward Avila's Harmony Villa Trailer Park. Might as well get this over with, she thought. Although she knew Kim Avila, whose parents owned the park, she hoped she wouldn't see her. She tried to think of a reasonable excuse for being there.

At the trailer park she saw some small children playing in the picnic area out front. They didn't pay any attention to her. The light was beginning to fade. She had some trouble making out the numbers on the parking spaces. At last, toward the rear of the park, she found number 22. A light was on inside the trailer.

She took a deep breath and walked up to the door. She knocked.

"Who is it?" a deep, male voice asked.

"Is Art there?" she asked. She thought her voice sounded squeaky.

A young man looked out through the screen door. "I'm Art."

He looks nice enough, she thought. "I, uh...I have something to give to you."

He opened the screen door.

She took the package from her bag and held it out to him.

As he reached for it, he smiled. "What's your name?"

She swallowed. "Christy."

"Well, Christy, would you like to come in?" he asked

as he took the package.

"Uh, no thanks. I've got to be going."

"I think you'd better come in," he said. He took something from his pocket and showed it to her. "I'm Deputy Art Wilson with the Lake County Sheriff's Department."

Christy stared at the badge in his hand. She felt her knees turn to rubber. She burst into tears. Deputy Wilson reached down and guided her into the trailer.

There were two other sheriff's deputies inside. One of them was a woman. She gave Christy some kleenex and told her to calm down. "It will be a lot easier for you if you cooperate with us," she said.

Meanwhile the other officers had opened the package. "It's the real thing," said Deputy Wilson. "Call in and tell them they can round up our other young friend."

He turned to Christy. "Why don't you tell us where you got this? Make it easy on yourself." Christy cried harder.

"Okay, let's go. We can stop by your house on the way. We're going to have to turn you over to the juvenile authorities."

An hour later Christy sat in a small office at the Lake County Sheriff's Department.

She had been talking with a juvenile probation officer. Her Uncle Roger was at the front desk talking

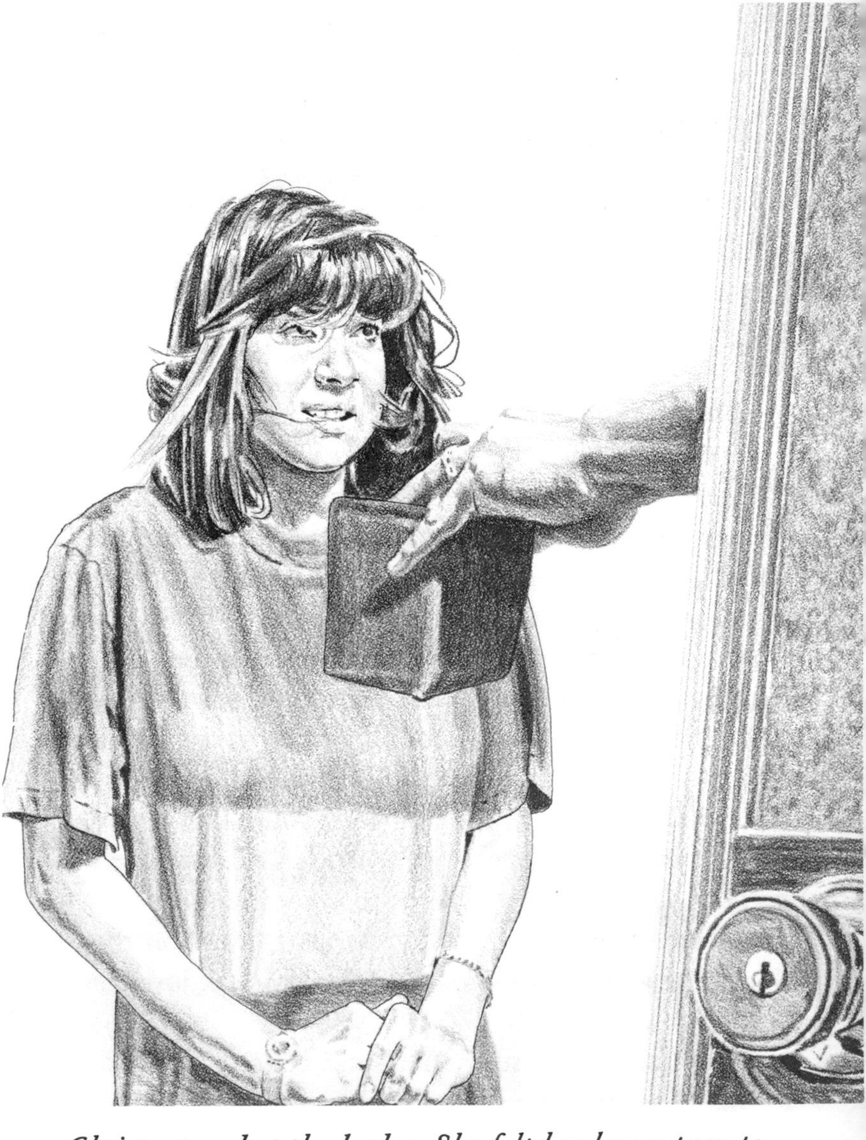

Christy stared at the badge. She felt her knees turn to rubber.

to a deputy. He was waiting to take her home after she'd been "processed" by the juvenile authorities.

Christy still hadn't said anything about Eric. She didn't want to be a narc. She couldn't believe he'd actually sold pot to an undercover cop! Maybe I could just mention Tom Rice, she thought. But then they still might get Eric.

Her dilemma was resolved by the appearance of Eric himself. She stared at him.

"Hi, Christy," he said. "Sorry about this."

She shook her head. Sorry, she thought with disgust. Well, at least he had the decency to admit it was his fault.

As it turned out, Eric told the deputies that Christy was just doing him a favor. He also told them he'd gotten the marijuana from Tom Rice. He told them everything he could in the hope that it would make things easier on him. That night, several marijuana dealers were arrested in and around Harmony Lake.

"At least you're getting a good newspaper story out of it," Christy said to Uncle Roger as he drove back to Harmony Lake. She tried to smile through her tears.

He shook his head. "I can't believe you, Christy Ann Jacobs. I don't know what your mother's going to say about this. Honestly, I thought you had more sense."

"Uncle Roger, do you *have* to tell her?"

"Of course. In fact, she may have to come up here

for the hearing on Wednesday. I'm going to talk to the sheriff on Monday and see what we need to do."

"I'm really sorry, Uncle Roger. Truly. I don't know why I did that. I just...When Eric asked me, I wanted to say no, but..." She sniffed and brushed at her tears. "I knew it was wrong, I just didn't know how to say no. I was afraid he'd stop liking me."

"I know it's hard to learn to speak up for what you believe," said Uncle Roger. "Especially if you want to impress somebody. It's one of life's harder lessons."

Christy snuffled into the kleenex. She was thinking about what her mother and stepfather would say. She prayed they wouldn't make her come home.

She moaned again. "Oh no, I just had the most horrible thought."

Her uncle glanced at her. "What's that?"

"Wednesday. The hearing. They're going to shoot my scene Wednesday or Thursday. I might miss it. My chance for fame. My lucky break! It could all go down the tubes!"

She stared at the road ahead. You blew it this time, she thought.

THE END

Thursday was the day that Christy's scene in *Last Chance Lake* was going to be filmed. Wednesday night she was so excited she could hardly sleep. She got up at six and fixed her hair. She redid her makeup four times.

"How long did you say your scene was?" Aunt Sylvia asked. She tried to keep a straight face as she handed Christy a piece of toast.

"Well, I think I can stretch it to 30 seconds if I speak real slowly," Christy said. "Oh, Aunt Sylvia, I can't eat this. I'm too nervous."

"Eat," her aunt commanded. "You need to keep your strength up."

At 9:00, Christy reported to the make-up trailer. Heather went with her. There, they took off all of Christy's makeup and started over. They messed up her hair and sprayed it into position. "You're supposed to have a windblown look," they said.

Christy and Heather walked over to the main dock to wait for Christy's scene to be called. "Oh, look!" cried Heather, clutching Christy's arm. "It's him!"

Although Sean Harris, the movie idol, had been in town several days, no one had seen much of him. The scenes he'd been shooting were on the other side of the lake. And when he was in town, he stayed in his room.

Uncle Roger wanted to interview him for the newspaper. But the opportunity hadn't come up yet.

"Oh, Aunt Sylvia, I can't eat. I'm too nervous," Christy moaned.

Now here he was, not more than ten feet away. Lois Kahn spotted Christy and motioned for her to come over. "Your scene is up in about an hour, Christy. Sean's going to take a break after this. Then we'll be ready."

"You mean my scene is with Sean?" Christy asked, unbelieving.

"Of course. Didn't you know that?"

Christy moaned. "I had no idea. I thought I was nervous *before.* Now I'll probably *expire* before I get a chance to be famous."

"Why don't you take her somewhere," said Lois to Heather, "and help her calm down?"

Heather pulled Christy away from the dock. They walked down the beach. "I've got an idea," Heather said, taking something from her pocket. "Why don't you have a couple hits of this? It will help you calm down, I'm sure."

Christy was surprised to see Heather with a joint, but she didn't show her feelings.

"Oh, I don't think so," she said. "I don't know what it might do."

"Okay," said Heather. "But I'm gonna have some." She lit the joint. They walked along in silence.

"Do you smoke much?" Christy asked. "How come you didn't tell me?"

"Well, I haven't done it very much. At first I wasn't sure how you'd feel. Then I saw you were cool about it. So that's why I brought this out."

"Oh," said Christy. She was thinking maybe she'd have just a teeny bit of the pot. Maybe it would take the edge off her nervousness.

"I don't know, though," Heather went on. "Now it might be harder to get it since Eric and Tom and those other people got busted."

Christy shook her head. She was still in shock at the news. Tom and Eric and some other people had been arrested the previous weekend for selling or growing marijuana.

"Doesn't that worry you?" she asked. "I mean, what if *you* got busted?"

"I'm real careful," said Heather. "And I'd *never* deal."

"But you can get arrested just for having it," Christy said. "C'mon, we'd better get back." They turned and started back toward the dock.

"You sure you don't want some?" Heather asked. "It's really relaxing."

Christy hesitated. Just a little bit might help, she thought. So I don't totally fall apart in front of Sean Harris. She looked at Heather. Nothing weird seemed to have happened to her.

Heather paused and started to put out the joint.

What did Christy do?

Choice A
*If you think Christy decided to smoke
some marijuana,*
turn to page 62.

Choice B
If you think Christy decided not *to
smoke marijuana,*
turn to page 65.

"Wait a second," Christy said. "Just a little ..."

She didn't feel any change after one puff. So she ended up taking three or four. "Wow!" she said after a few minutes, "Now I feel it."

They walked in silence. "Oh, I really feel it," she said. Then, "Did I already say that?"

"Oh, Christy, I think you're stoned," said Heather.

"No, I'm not," said Christy. "Not very. Listen, I can remember my lines...wait a second, I'll get it...Okay, here goes. 'Yeah, I saw her last night at Tiny's Grill. She was with some older guy I thought was her...' No, wait a minute, okay. 'I saw her at Tiny's Grill last night...' This stuff is pretty strange."

She took a small slip of paper from her pocket and read the words. "I saw her last night at Tiny's grill. She was with some old guy. I thought maybe he was her father." She stuffed the paper back into her pocket and tried her lines a few more times.

When they got back to the dock, Christy still wasn't sure she had them down. "How're we doing?" Lois asked her.

"Fine," said Christy. "I hope."

"Okay. You just go with Marty here and she'll show you where you're supposed to be."

Marty Freeman led Christy to the end of the dock. "Sit here," she said, "and hold this pole like you're fishing. Sean's going to come around there in a boat. We'll do the scene several times, from different angles. We'll do your lines and Sean's lines but not necessarily in order. I'll cue you when it's your turn. Got it?"

Christy nodded, but she wasn't sure exactly what Marty had said. She heard someone say "action." She saw the boat with Sean Harris approaching. He was looking at her. Then he was looking at the camera. "...She has blond hair. She's a reporter for the *Times Express*. She was wearing a red jacket. Do you know who I mean?"

Christy felt paralyzed. She looked at Marty. Marty smiled and nodded. "I saw her at Tiny's last night," she blurted out. "With an older guy. I mean with an old guy..." She stopped and looked helplessly at Marty.

"That's okay, honey," Marty said, "but keep going. We'll be doing it again."

They did it again. And again. And again. Each time Christy failed to get it right. Her memory just didn't seem to work even when Marty told her exactly what to say.

"What's the matter with this chick?" asked Sean Harris in disgust.

"We've spent enough time on this scene," the director said. "Let's wait and see what we've got. Then we'll decide if we can use it or not."

Christy felt the tears beginning to come. "I'm so sorry," she mumbled. "I don't know what's wrong."

"It's okay, honey." Marty patted her shoulder. "It happens sometimes."

Christy walked up the dock. Heather was waiting for her. Steve was there too. "How'd it go?" Heather asked excitedly.

Christy did some serious crying then. "I blew it," she wailed. "I couldn't get my part straight. I kept spacing it out."

"Oh no," said Heather.

"And my scene will probably be cut out of the movie. And Sean Harris thinks I'm an idiot." I'll never smoke that stuff again, she thought. I never want to make myself so stupid again.

Steve handed her a handkerchief. "Thanks." She blew her nose.

He put his arms around her and patted her back. She sniffed into his shirt. Hmm, this isn't too bad, she thought after a while. She rested her cheek against his shoulder.

"All better?" he asked, stepping back to look at her.

"Not quite." She burrowed into his shoulder again.

"Maybe it'll work out," he said. "Maybe it's not as bad as you think."

"Maybe," she said. "But I doubt it."

THE END

Nope, Christy thought. Too risky. I'll just have to be my scared-to-death self. She went over her lines in her mind.

"How're we doing?" Lois asked her when they got back to the dock.

"Actually, I'm about to die of fright," Christy said.

Lois laughed. "That's normal. You'll be fine. You go with Marty now and she'll show you where you're supposed to be."

Marty Freeman led Christy to the end of the dock. "Sit here," she said, "and hold this pole like you're fishing. Sean's going to come around there in a boat. We'll do the scene several times, from several different angles. We'll do your lines and Sean's lines but not necessarily in order. I'll cue you when it's your turn. Got it?"

Christy nodded. I guess I've got it, she thought. She looked around for the boat with Sean Harris in it.

"Action," someone said. The boat came around the end of the dock.

Sean Harris was looking at her. Then he looked at the camera. "Excuse me," he said. "They told me you work at the restaurant here. I'm looking for a woman, Margaret Davies. She has blond hair. She's a reporter for the *Times Express*. She was wearing a red jacket. Do you know who I mean?"

Christy took a deep breath. She looked at Marty, who nodded and smiled. "I saw her last night..." she began.

For a split second her mind went blank. Then she remembered and finished her short speech.

Then she did it again. Then Sean did his part again. Then she did hers once more. "Cut," the director called for the last time. He gave Christy a brief smile.

"Nice work," Marty said. "Thanks, honey."

Christy smiled with relief. She glanced at Sean. He caught her eye and winked. "Good job," he said.

Christy could barely keep her feet on the dock as she headed back toward Heather. Steve was waiting too. "How'd it go?" Heather asked excitedly.

"Oh, okay, I guess," she said casually. Then she let out a shriek. She grabbed Steve and Heather around their necks and jumped up and down. "It was so far out! I was so great! I was so scared. And he winked at me. Oh, I can't believe it. Sean Harris winked at me." She stopped and looked closely at Steve. "You're not jealous, are you?"

Steve laughed. He shook his head. "You're crazy," he said. Then he hugged her. "But you're cute."

*   *   *

Two weeks later, the filming was done. To celebrate, the cast held a big party in the hotel restaurant. Uncle Roger, as a member of the press, was invited. Aunt Sylvia, Jon, Heather, and Carrie were there too. So was

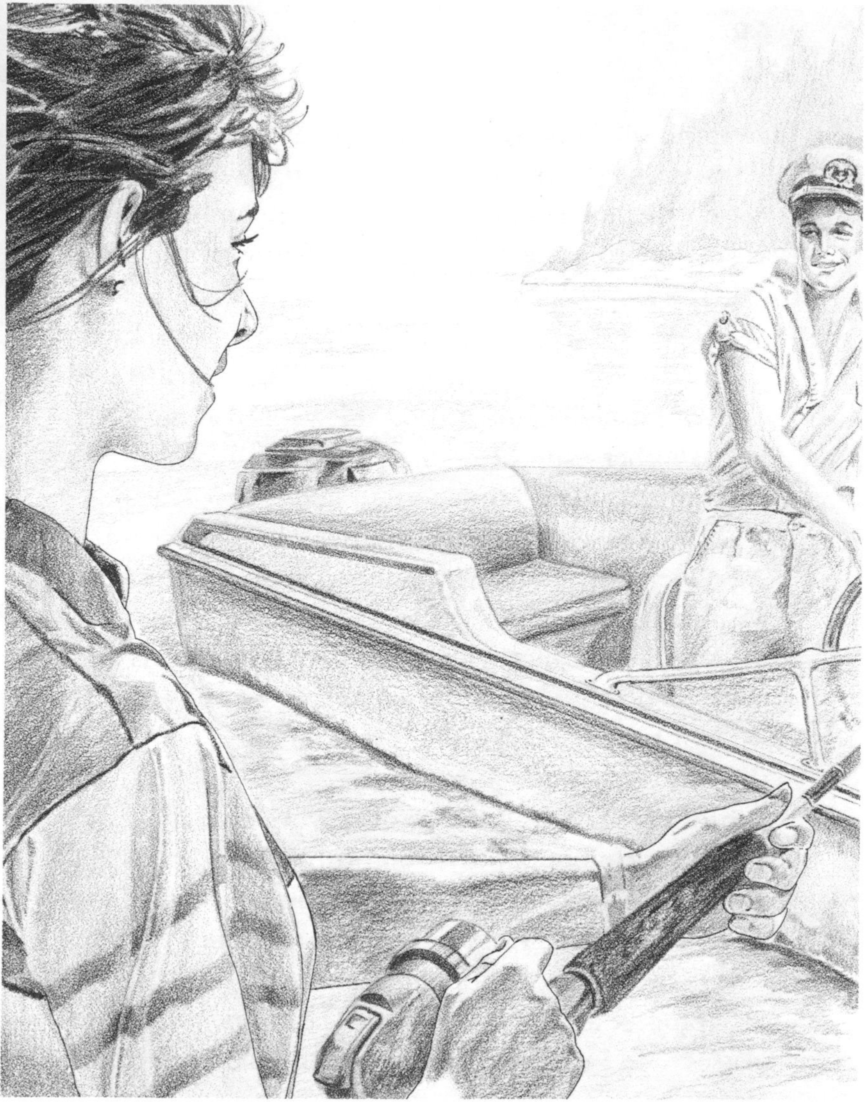

Christy glanced at Sean. He caught her eye and winked. "Good job," he said.

everyone who'd been in the movie. Steve had come as Christy's guest. And of course, Andrew, whose family owned the hotel, was there. In fact, thought Christy, as she looked around, it looks like most of the town is here.

Christy sat with Steve, Heather, Jon, Amy, and Todd.

"So did you really meet Sean?" Amy asked.

"Not exactly," Christy said. "He winked at me once. And another time he said, 'Hi, Cathy.' "

"I talked to him some," said Todd. "He's okay."

"I think he's kind of stuck on himself," said Heather. "We met Josie Lansing though. She was real sweet, wasn't she, Christy?"

"Mmm. Real nice. A normal person. Like Lois and Marty and some of the other people on the crew."

"Not typical Hollywood," said Todd.

"Whatever *that* is," said Steve.

Andrew brought a bottle of sparkling cider over to the table. He popped the top off like an expert. Half the contents foamed out and ran down his arm. They all held out their glasses for what remained.

"Oh, well, it's the thought that counts," said Christy.

"I propose a toast," said Todd. The group raised their glasses. "To Harmony Lake and Hollywood—partners forever."

"Hear, hear."

"To show business," said Heather.

"To monkey business," added Steve.

They all sipped from their glasses.

"I want to make one more toast," said Christy. "To friends. And cousins. And Steve. To the best summer I've ever had."

THE END

About this Book

Christy's Chance is part of an important new series of books designed to help young people make informed, responsible decisions about drug use. Other books in the series include *Serena's Secret* and *Danny's Dilemma*. They combine substance abuse information and models for resisting peer pressure in the popular interactive adventure book format.

The development of these books was supported by funds from the National Institute of Child Health and Development. They have gone through extensive pretesting with preadolescents and have been carefully reviewed by substance abuse professionals. The committee of professionals not only gave initial input to determine appropriate content, but also reviewed the books during their development.

About the Authors

Christine DeVault and Bryan Strong, PhD, are educators who have authored numerous elementary, middle school and college texts in sociology, psychology and family life.

Also available as part of this series are three companion nonfiction books, *Alcohol: The Real Story, Tobacco: The Real Story,* and *Marijuana: The Real Story.* Each book provides up-to-date facts and information about the use and abuse of alcohol, tobacco and marijuana. They are compact, easy to read and reinforced with illustrations and challenging case study scenarios.